All That Matters

- 2nd Edition

Loralee Lillibridge

Printed by
Tell-Tale Publishing Group, LLC
5174 Peri Street
Swartz Creek, MI 48473
www.tell-talepublishing.com

Dahlia Imprint
DAHLIA

Sincere thanks and deep appreciation to everyone at Tell-Tale Publishing for your belief in this project and making it happen.

To the country singers whose ballads inspired this story — Your music says what a heart needs to hear.

Heartfelt thanks to my awesome critique group for continuing to push me to stretch my writing boundaries.

This one's for y'all!

Chapter One

"**P**lease let him be here."

Whatever crazy stunts she'd pulled in the past, this one topped them all and Faith Morgan was scared Buddy Lee Walker wouldn't answer his door. Wouldn't help her this time.

Standing at the back door of the small tract-house where Buddy Lee had lived since they were kids in high school, Faith experienced a *déjà vu* moment. The last time she'd been here, her daddy had come storming after her, horrified that his daughter was mingling with the town's *white trash*. His words, not hers.

Like the good friend he was, Buddy Lee took the blame that time without ever revealing the real reason she'd been there. Now after six years, here she was at his door again, hoping with all her heart his friendship still held.

Balling her fist, she pounded again as hard as she could. As much as she hated to ask him for help, Buddy Lee was the only one she could turn to. The only one who understood the reasons behind her rebellious teen years.

He'd been her stalwart champion, despite her father's disapproval. The protective brother she'd never had.

But that was then. This was now. She was twenty-three, not seventeen. She was responsible for her own actions. Or should be. What would he think of her now?

"Buddy Lee, please answer the door!"

A heart-stopping thought hit her. What if he didn't live here any longer? Or was married? She'd been living forty miles away in Granite City ever since she moved there after graduating from college. Close enough for the obligatory, yet infrequent, visits home to check on her mother's health. Her high school protector had been all but forgotten. Until now.

"Buddy Lee, I need you!" She raised her hand one more time. Just one more try, then she'd leave.

Buddy Lee Walker didn't appreciate the late-night knocking that interrupted his favorite *Gunsmoke* rerun, especially since he suspected the unwelcome visitor was only Scooter Craddock on his way home from his shift at the GAS'N GO. The persistent banging on the door grew louder over the noise of the marshal's gunfight.

Even though he'd seen the classic TV Western many times, Buddy Lee punched up the volume even louder, so as not to miss any action when Miss Kitty came down the staircase in the Long Branch. He jogged down the hall to the kitchen, flipping on the light switch as he passed. "All right, all right, I'm on my way. Hold your horses, for cryin' out loud."

He yanked open the back door, ready to ask Scooter what his damn problem was, but nearly swallowed his tongue instead when he saw the shadowed figure standing there.

"What the...Faith?" Buddy Lee's heart slammed against his ribs so hard he had to grab the doorframe to keep from falling flat out when his legs suddenly went boneless. He had to be dreaming, because the girl in those dreams stood there with tears streaming down her face, gulping great big sobs between words Buddy Lee couldn't make heads nor tails of. And she was a full-fledged woman, for cryin' out loud! The high-voltage charge that ripped through his body made the hairs on the back of his neck stand straight up. He shivered like someone had walked on his grave.

"I yelled and yelled, Buddy Lee. Didn't you hear me? C...can I come in? Please? I don't know where else to go."

Faith Morgan was the last person Buddy Lee ever expected to see at his back door—or any door, for that matter—but the outright fear in her eyes told him this wasn't a social call. Now, why did that tie his insides in knots?

"Hey...hey, don't cry. C'mon in." Puzzled, and more than a little shocked, he took her arm and drew her inside, giving the door a shove behind him with one bare foot, but not before he shot a cautious glance up and down the street.

"Tell me what's wrong, Faith. Are you hurt?" His imagination conjured up a thousand reasons for her appearance, but they were all fantasies. Not a logical one in the bunch.

"I'm in trouble, Buddy Lee." Tear-bright green eyes held him captive. "I can't marry Royce and I need you to help me."

Her plea hit the soft place in Buddy Lee's heart. A place where he'd kept her memory hidden for oh so many years. But her last statement threw Buddy Lee's brain into shock.

"What do you mean you can't marry him? You're kidding, right?" He did a quick math calculation. "Today's Monday. Your wedding is Saturday morning. What's the problem?"

Even though he hadn't seen Faith in a long time, he knew about her engagement to Royce Webb, her father's right-hand man at the bank. Their upcoming nuptials had been the main topic of gossip in the tight-knit community for the past couple of months. Oh, yeah, he knew all right.

Buddy Lee kept asking her questions while he steered her down the hall toward the living room, kicking his discarded boots and socks out of the way as they went. He jerked a dirty work shirt off the doorknob, tossed it into the bedroom, and yanked the door shut. Shoot, he hadn't expected company. Especially not her. Not in a million years.

"Here, sit right here." He fumbled to rid the sofa of a pile of old newspapers, the last three issues of *Classic Cars* magazines and a couple of articles of clothing he didn't particularly care to have Faith see. He tossed the whole mess on the floor behind the sofa and patted the faded, blue plaid cushion, the imprint of its last occupant still obvious in the way it dipped and sagged. Funny, he'd never noticed how worn-out the furniture looked until now.

The shock of seeing Faith in his living room was rendering him speechless. He couldn't believe she was actually right here—right now. And that set his mind racing with a long list of reasons as to why. None of them made a lick of sense.

Faith finally sat and he hunkered down on one knee beside her. "Look, Faith, I hate to keep asking the same question, but what's going on? Why aren't you marrying Royce?"

Trying to keep his voice steady was almost impossible, since his heart kept pounding like an out-of-sync piston. He looked down to make sure the thing hadn't jumped out of his chest, then zeroed in on Faith's face. Big mistake.

She must've been crying for some time, because her eyes were all puffy and red and she kept sniffling until finally, he reached in his back pocket for his handkerchief, checked to make sure it was clean and handed it to her. "Here."

"Buddy Lee," Faith whispered between hiccups and sobs and wiping her nose with his handkerchief.

"Yeah, what is it, Faith?" He held his breath. Oh, man, if she didn't tell him what was wrong pretty soon, he was gonna explode.

"I just didn't...I mean, there's no one else I can trust." She blew her nose real loud, then gave him a pleading look that tugged at his unprotected heart something fierce.

A lock of cinnamon-brown hair fell across her cheek and stuck in the damp track of her tears. Without thinking, he reached up to tuck it behind her ear, caught off guard when the wayward strand's silky texture rasped against his rough fingers. The seductive sensation made him want things he knew he shouldn't. Of their own accord, his knuckles skimmed across her soft cheek as he withdrew his shaking hand.

"You can always talk to me, Faith. You know that." He eased up and sat next to her, real careful not to sit too close.

Since he was a good deal taller than Faith, he had to hunch over to hear what she was saying. The urge to put his arms around her was eating him up. He'd never so much as hugged her in all the years he'd known her. Not that he hadn't wanted to, because he reckoned he'd loved Faith Morgan for about two forevers. That was something he'd never told anyone, not even Scooter and especially not Faith.

Wasn't going to, either. That's what was making it so hard to keep from reaching for her now.

"Look, Faith, if you're in trouble, I need to know what it is. Otherwise, how am I gonna help you?" He was slipping back in time, barely hanging on to his good sense. Knowing Faith had been the only good thing in his life when he was seventeen. Rescuing her from her daddy's wrath so many times made him feel like he amounted to something besides white trash, but Faith left town after graduation, and he accepted the fact that those good feelings were a thing of the past.

Even though she'd been a rule-breaker as a teen, landing in hot water time after time, one significant fact of life never changed. Faith was fancy—the daughter of the town banker—and right up there in Liberty's small, but oh so proper society.

Buddy Lee was about as far from fancy as a man could get. He was Boyd Walker's son, a fact that made him mad as hell. It set his teeth on edge when folks in town called him "Boyd's boy." He hadn't been anybody's damn *boy* since his mama died when he was six.

The thought that Faith's daddy might be headed over here looking for her grabbed his attention right then. Having a set-to with the likes of Lionel Morgan sure wasn't on his list of things he wanted for Christmas. Not that he believed in Santa Claus. Definitely not with Morgan's bank holding the mortgage on his struggling auto repair shop. No way. Santa never came to this side of the tracks.

"C'mon, Faith, tell me what's wrong so I can help you," he pleaded, anxious to get on with solving whatever was causing her grief.

All the wild escapades he'd rescued her from during their high school years flashed through his confused brain like a movie trailer. Lord only knew what she'd gotten into now. He'd taken the blame for her pranks more than once to save her from her daddy's wrath. Easy enough to do when your own daddy was behind bars for robbery and a bungled shoot-out. Everyone in Liberty expected the worst from "that Walker kid."

Now here she was asking for his help again. Well, shoot. He'd always been a sucker for those soft green eyes and that "help-me-this-time-Buddy Lee-and-I-promise-I'll-never-do-it-again" smile. But, they weren't kids any longer. So why did he have the feeling he was about to do something stupid?

Then, without warning, she surprised the hell out of him by launching herself into his arms, and he didn't know where to put them, except around her. A groan of pure pleasure rumbled up from somewhere deep inside his body. He closed his eyes in surrender, figuring he'd landed smack in the middle of Paradise.

In his wildest dreams, he hadn't imagined how soft she would feel or how naturally she would fit into the curve of his arms. Couldn't have imagined it in a hundred years. If death claimed him right now, just two weeks shy of his twenty-fifth birthday, he figured he'd die a happy man, sitting right there with Faith curled up against his chest. It was such a fine feeling, he screwed up enough courage to rest his chin on the top of her head and lose himself in the scent of her apple blossom shampoo.

But when her lips moved against the sensitive skin right there where his neck met his collarbone and her whispered words reached his ears, his world crumbled like a clod of dirt under a boot heel.

"Say you'll marry me, Buddy Lee. We have to tell them the baby is yours."

"We *what?*" His words struggled out at two octaves higher than normal, and his eyes crossed like he'd been smacked upside the head with a two-by-four. His ears started ringing louder than the bell down at the fire station. When his breath bunched up in his throat so thick he nearly choked on it, he *whooshed* it out, then dragged in fresh air until his lungs promised not to shut down on him. He couldn't believe what he was hearing. "What baby, Faith? Whose baby? Tell who?"

He held her at arm's length, searching her tear-streaked face for a sensible explanation to her very un-sensible announcement. When she flinched and looked away he realized he had a death grip on her arms and released them in such a hurry, she swayed back against the sofa. Shame stung him when he saw the faint red marks his fingers had left on her skin.

He mumbled an apology, still reeling from her words. Marry her? Maybe in his dreams. But, a baby? Never.

"Please, Buddy Lee, say you will. I promise this will be the last time I ask you for help. Honestly."

"Now, wait a minute, Faith." His mind was back-pedaling faster than he could keep up. "You'd better tell me about this baby first. And what about Royce? I thought your wedding was all set for Saturday."

He'd been hearing about the coming event from everyone in town for the last two months. Cripes, didn't those people have anything else to talk about?

She sat there hugging herself, looking at him in that heart-melting way she'd always had of making him feel like a jerk to even consider saying "no" to anything she asked.

"Oh, it is. Daddy's got all the arrangements made. Every single thing." Faith fidgeted, glanced toward the front door, then back at him. Her eyes glistened with more tears ready to fall. "But..."

His heart plummeted to his feet. *Uh-oh. That could only mean one thing.* The thought of Faith and Royce doing *it*, even if they were engaged, caused a wallop of plain ol' envy to butt heads with his good sense before he managed to speak.

"You're not the first expectant bride to ever walk down the aisle, Faith. Is that your big problem?" He moved to curve his arm around her, drawing her closer. Tried to sound sympathetic when what he really wanted to do was let go with a flying fist into the wall.

"I'll bet ol' Royce is proud as a peacock about being a daddy," he said, surprised he could even manage to talk with his jaws locked up like they were.

Something about the funny little noise she made in the back of her throat and the way she screwed up her face set off a warning bell in his head. "You did tell him, didn't you?"

She shook her head, coppery curls swaying. "No," she whispered. "I can't let him find out. I don't want to marry him. I won't."

When she turned her face upwards so that her green eyes met his, there was no mistaking the flash of defiance burning brightly in their depths. Oh, boy, he'd seen that warning spark on more than one occasion, right before she did something wild and crazy just to break her daddy's rules. That streak of rebelliousness coupled with her innocent charm had beguiled him then and held him spellbound now. There was no accounting for the way his heart worked.

"I can't explain everything to you yet, Buddy Lee, but I will soon. Just trust me for now, please?"

A queasy feeling suddenly roiled through his stomach in giant waves. This was *not* looking good.

"Trust you? Darlin', if I remember right, every time I trusted you I landed up to my ass in alligators." He rubbed a hand over his face as old memories kicked in. "Keeping you out of trouble with your daddy when we were in high school was a full-time job. Those crazy pranks of yours nearly got me expelled more than once.

"I didn't mind taking the blame back then, but this idea is *waaaay* too wild. Much as I'd like to, I can't afford to fight those particular 'gators anymore."

He wasn't about to give Lionel Morgan a reason to call in the bank note. He could just imagine the banker's delight if that happened. But his resolve started slipping the minute Faith reached for his hand. Awww, hell.

"Maybe you'd better start at the beginning," he said with a sigh, hoping there weren't too many alligators lurking in this particular swamp.

Faith took a deep breath before she spoke, and he detected a slight tremor in her voice.

"About three weeks ago I came to town to bring some of my things to the new house," she said. "Royce planned to meet me there. We had furniture being delivered and wanted to make sure everything was what we'd ordered."

She stopped to blow her nose. "He'd gotten there early and put all the furniture in place. He even had wine and flowers waiting. Soft music on the new sound system we'd had installed. It...it was perfect. You know, romantic?"

The little hitch in her voice was enough to melt him right down to his socks. If he'd been wearing any.

"It's okay, darlin', just take your time." The endearment slipped out before he could stop it.

She sighed. "At first, I didn't realize he'd been drinking. We had some wine, danced a bit. Kissed a lot." A pink flush stained her cheeks. "He kept insisting the wedding was only weeks away and...well...things just happened. I honestly believed I was in love with him, Buddy Lee. Thought he loved me, too." Something between a laugh and a sob escaped her lips. "You probably think I'm making this up, don't you? Twenty-three years old and not smart enough to insist on protected sex." Her eyes filled and she blinked hard. "I've been such a fool. Royce isn't the man I fell in love with. That man was a gentleman. He treated me special. Surprised me with gifts I should've known he couldn't afford. Even Daddy was impressed with his financial background, but now I wonder how much of that was true. I think he's in some kind of trouble, Buddy Lee. How can I marry a man who lies to me? And his violent temper frightens me. I just don't trust him."

Buddy Lee pulled her trembling body close so she could bury her face against the curve of his shoulder, willing himself not to think about her nearness, her softness. *Impossible.* This was Faith, right here in his arms. With her tremors vibrating through his own body, the heady sensation of their hearts thudding together so perfectly sent shafts of desire to places he'd already labeled off-limits.

He was angry and didn't understand why. He had no right. Faith and Royce were getting married. It wasn't his business whether they had sex before or after their wedding. Hell, *after* would probably be unique in this day and age.

"I guess I don't see what this has to do with me, Faith." He cupped her chin to turn her face toward his and looked deep in her eyes. Wanted to disappear in their emerald depths. *Hold on, Walker. Don't go getting any ideas.* He rearranged his thoughts. "Look, you're gonna have a baby, and Royce is the father. You're getting married Saturday. One and one makes three. Simple math." *Simple, hell.* Every word left a bitter taste in his mouth.

"There's more," Faith said, her voice soft and full of emotion. "More than you can imagine. The reason I can't marry him."

He swallowed hard, wondering how the hell a football had gotten stuck in his throat. "Tell me, then."

"You know those home-pregnancy tests? Well, I took one earlier in the week. I was nervous about telling Royce the results, because I wasn't sure how he felt about having a family so soon. Then I realized there were a lot of things I didn't know about him and started having second thoughts about the wedding." She looked at him expectantly.

Well, shoot. Did she think he had an answer? So far, he was still in a fog as to his part in the scheme Faith was cooking up. Nothing seemed too irregular except the fact that she was upset about having a baby.

"Okay, so you're pregnant by a few weeks. Your wedding dress will still fit, won't it?"

Faith punched his arm. "You're not listening, Buddy Lee Walker."

"I am, too. Honest." Lord, save him from teary-eyed, pregnant women. He was convinced Faith's emotional upheaval was just the result of her condition. He wasn't convinced if *he* was happy with that conclusion or not. He was afraid there was more. Sure enough, there was.

"Tonight I was in the bedroom unpacking and didn't hear Royce drive up." She sniffled, then continued. "When I opened one of the dresser drawers, there was a gun. A real gun, Buddy Lee, sticking out from under some of Royce's socks. And a big bundle of money. Lots of it." Fear widened her eyes. "There were some papers, too, but I didn't get a chance to look at them."

He couldn't stand to see her so afraid. This wasn't a joke, after all. Something was definitely wrong here. Talk about a swamp full of 'gators. "What the hell was a gun and money doing in a sock drawer? What did Royce say?"

"When he came in the room, I was holding the money. I didn't want to touch the gun, but he knew I'd seen it. He wouldn't tell me where the money came from or why he had a gun. I mean, I know it's perfectly normal to have permits for guns, but I just didn't want any in our home. Not with children around. I tried to reason with him, but he grabbed the money out of my hand, slammed the drawer shut and shoved me out of the room." She shuddered, took a deep breath.

"I've never seen him so angry, Buddy Lee. There was no reason for him to scare me like that. So when he refused to explain about the money and acted so strange when I asked about the papers, I told him I wanted to postpone the wedding. I had the craziest premonition that there was something really wrong about the whole situation."

A flash of fury whipped through him. Something bad was going on, no doubt about it. "What do you mean? What kind of premonition?"

"I wasn't really accusing him of anything," she said, "but I know what his salary is at the bank. There was a lot more money in that drawer than he could've ever saved on what he makes. Big bills, too. And besides, he'd borrowed money from me in the past when he was between paychecks. We talked about how his upcoming promotion would help us financially. He had big plans for becoming an investment advisor." Her deep breath turned into a shudder, and she had to wait a minute before continuing.

"His anger was so unexpected. So frightening. He flew into a rage and then I yelled back." She made a weak gesture with her shoulders. "You know how I get sometimes. Well, one word led to another. The next thing I knew, we were having a shouting match. That's when he slapped me. Said I'd be sorry if I didn't keep my mouth shut. He even threatened to shut me up permanently."

Her tears fell freely, and she swiped at them with the already-damp handkerchief. "There was no way I was going to tell him I carried his child. Not after that. So I just ran. Even forgot my car and...and, well, here I am." She heaved a big sigh and ducked her head. "I'm really scared this time."

Then she pulled away and unbuttoned her blouse. Buddy Lee watched in stunned silence as it slid from her shoulders. What he saw turned his stomach.

"Awww, Faith, no," he groaned.

He didn't consider himself a violent man, but the dark purple blotches and tell-tale scratches streaking across her soft skin made him want to smash his fist into Royce Webb's face until he no longer felt this red-hot anger. *Son. Of. A. Bitch.*

Gently, he moved her hands aside and fastened her blouse, taking care that his clumsy movements didn't inflict more pain. She was so fragile, so lovely. A sudden wave of tenderness surged through him and he felt his heart crack. It took him all of two seconds to make up his mind and the hell with anyone who tried to stop him.

"Tell me what you need me to do, darlin'," he whispered. Bending forward, he dared to touch his lips to her forehead. Her shaky sigh as she leaned into his embrace threatened to tear his heart right from his chest.

"Just marry me and be my baby's daddy for now."

Her words were warm against his chest and adrenalin shot through his veins like a good slug of 150-proof. That was all he needed. He got to his feet, pulling Faith with him. Whatever had to be done, he'd do it to protect her. But he still had questions.

"Are you planning to do this without telling your folks? Your daddy won't expect you to go through with the wedding if you tell him what happened, will he?"

Faith's mouth quivered and damned if all the blood in Buddy Lee's head didn't rush south again.

"Daddy won't believe me. He'll just say I'm trying to make trouble. You know how he is. And if he finds out about the baby, he'll force me to marry Royce. That's why we have to tell them the baby is yours."

Buddy Lee looked at her sweet face and decided he might as well find out what he'd wanted to know for a long time. "Do you love him? Royce, I mean?" His insides started icing up while he waited for her answer.

She touched his face, the soft pads of her fingertips barely skimming his cheek. Her voice lowered to a murmur. "No, I never did. I realize now, I just wanted someone to love me."

Oh, damn, he was dying here. "Won't he figure it out? If you were only, um, together once," he stumbled over the phrase he didn't want to think about, "it'd be easy enough to count back and know the baby is his."

"That's why we have to say I'm already three months along." Faith still had her hand on his cheek. "I've got it all figured out. If Royce thinks I was pregnant before he and I uh...you know, then he'll believe the baby isn't his. And Daddy won't be able to do anything when he finds out you and I are already married."

Buddy Lee's poor mind was spinning like a tumbleweed caught in a dust devil. The only thing he was certain of was that he was about to be married to the girl of his dreams and her baby was gonna call him Daddy...if Lionel Morgan didn't blow him to Kingdom Come first.

"Well, there's no way I'm going to let you go back..."

The back door slammed and, instinctively, he stepped in front of her, placing himself between her and whatever threat might be headed their way. He had a feeling the alligators were ganging up on him.

Loralee Lillibridge

Chapter Two

"Hey, Walker, you still awake in there?"

The refrigerator door squeaked and Scooter's gravelly, three-pack-a-day voice bounced off the kitchen walls like hail on a tin roof.

Buddy Lee relaxed his guard, but kept himself between faith and the kitchen. As usual, his friend was helping himself to a cold one. Well, hell, was the whole damn town gonna show up at his back door tonight? He didn't want to deal with Scooter's inquisition right now. How the devil was he going to explain Faith being here? Might as well try to explain *space.*

Scooter ambled down the hall, the brown-bottled longneck almost to his mouth before he jerked to a stop right at the living room doorway. An unopened bag of corn chips dangled from his other hand. Wide, disbelieving eyes stared at Buddy Lee and Faith from behind over-sized, black rimmed glasses.

Buddy Lee could have kicked himself for not locking the back door after Faith had shown up. Scooter was better than the local newspaper when it came to circulating gossip in Liberty. His exaggerated version of the situation would be spread all over town by morning.

"Hot damn! What're you doin' here, Faith?" Scooter flopped down on a worn, rust-colored easy chair and poked his short, stubby legs out in front of him. He shot Buddy Lee a look that said, *What have you gotten yourself into this time, dude?* then chugged his beer like he was fighting off a serious case of dehydration. His appreciative "aahhh" followed the crackle of the bag of chips being ripped opened.

Buddy Lee fired off his own look that said, *Don't even go there if you know what's good for you.* Then he turned to Faith. "Maybe you'd better tell him." He'd leave it up to her. Yeah, that's what he'd do. He sure as hell couldn't explain something that still had his brain spinning U-ees inside his skull.

"Buddy Lee and I have to get married, Scooter." Faith sniffled a couple of times and dabbed at her eyes.

Jeez, if she started crying again he didn't know if he could handle it. Her tears pure-D tore him up. Then she reached for his hand and he felt ten feet tall.

"Y'all are just pullin' my leg, right?" Scooter pushed back the orange and blue GAS-'N-GOgimme cap resting on his fringe of mud-brown hair and scratched his head. "If I didn't know better, B.L., I'd bet a dollar you've been keeping company with ol' Jack Daniels." Resettling his cap, he proceeded to stuff another handful of corn chips in his mouth, chewing noisily.

"Your daddy know you're here, Faith?" Scooter asked after he'd swallowed, then chugged more beer. "I only wondered 'cause Royce was down at the pumps just before I closed up, looking mighty pissed. Took off like a tomcat with his tail on fire, after he gassed up that sporty car of his. Had some big guy with him who looked like he was kin to a gorilla. What's going on?" He plunged his hand back in the chip bag, bringing another handful to his mouth.

Buddy Lee leaned closer to Faith, wanting to hear her answer himself. Scooter's noisy chomping wasn't helping any.

"You know Daddy's not running my life, Scooter." Faith moved back to the lumpy sofa, pulling Buddy Lee with her. "I make my own decisions."

Scooter *haw-hawed* at that, spraying corn chip crumbs all over himself. "So, you an' Royce have a lovers' spat or what?" He brushed crumbs from his chin with stubby fingers, still chuckling. "Wedding jitters, right?" He slapped his knee and crowed again.

Clearly, Scooter thought this whole thing was a joke. If it was, Buddy Lee wished somebody would tell him the punch line.

"Like she said, we're getting married, pal." He emphasized each word, just in case Scooter had trouble hearing over his Frito-crunching.

"Yes," Faith said. "Tomorrow." She rested her hand on his knee and every nerve in his body jerked to attention. Oh, yeah. Every damn one.

Scooter's mouth fell open so wide you could've driven a Humvee in it and never touched the sides. "You're serious, ain'tcha?"

"She said so, didn't she?" Buddy Lee sat up straighter. Faith didn't lie. Well, maybe a few fibs as a kid. This proposed deception of hers was hard for him to accept, though, because what she had in mind was a good deal bigger than a fib.

"Promise you won't tell anyone yet," Faith said. "You'll ruin everything if you do."

"But...but, you an' Royce are getting married Saturday, right?" Scooter eyed Faith closely, then narrowed his gaze at Buddy Lee. "Walker, you better tell me what the hell's goin' on here."

Telling Scooter was as good as putting it on the six o'clock news. Buddy Lee could see it now. *"Wealthy banker's daughter weds up-to-his-ass-in-debt convict's son. Details at eleven."*

Details would be good, he thought, fully aware of the woman beside him. Like, right now. It wasn't that he didn't trust her. Shoot, he didn't know what to think. She'd appeared out of the blue and in a matter of minutes had thrown herself at him, proposed marriage and wanted him to claim to be the father of her child. When the real father was still around, probably madder'n hell. He blew out a deep sigh. Did she expect him to agree without even a second thought? He must be losing his everlovin' mind, because he knew that's what he was going to do, sure as Texas had Longhorns. *Scared* didn't even begin to describe his state of mind right now. *Crazy* might.

Then Faith smiled up at him and he was a goner. He didn't give a damn. He'd marry her tomorrow if that's what she wanted, and think about details later. A lot later. Right now, he had to get rid of Scooter and figure out what to do about her tonight.

Getting Scooter to leave was fairly simple. Buddy Lee bribed him with a new bag of corn chips and the last two issues of ON THE ROAD, Scoot's favorite auto magazine with lots of pictures, then hustled him out the back door. Convincing Faith to stay all night took a little more work.

"I can't put you out of your bed, Buddy Lee." Faith stood in the hall half an hour later, protesting his insistence that she sleep in his room.

"No problem," he assured her with a lot more confidence than he felt. "I'll sleep on the sofa. You can't go home all messed up like you are. Your mama would have a fit and your daddy...well...." Jeez, he didn't even want to think about what her daddy might do. She could argue all she wanted, but there was no way he was letting her leave now. For all they knew, Royce could be out there looking for her. So could her daddy. Or both of them. Buddy Lee swallowed hard.

Frantically, he tried to remember how long it had been since he'd laundered his sheets. Only a couple of days ago, he recalled, so he was pretty sure they didn't smell like motor oil. He couldn't change them. This was the only set he owned. "Dumb and Dumber" oughta be tattooed on his forehead.

"Then I'll sleep on the sofa," Faith said. "I don't mind, honestly."

"I'm not letting you sleep on the sofa, Faith, so just forget it." He didn't have any bedding for that and he couldn't expect her to sleep without any. He started scrambling around, grabbing his dirty work clothes from the corner of his bedroom and tossing them in the closet, while Faith kept on arguing. She always did talk too much.

His nerves were strung tighter than a fiddle string at the thought of her staying all night, and in her condition. Lord help him, if old man Morgan showed up before they got out of town there'd be more than hell to pay, and he was poorer than a church mouse already.

"Here, you can wear these," he said, shoving a handful of folded clothes at her and holding his breath until she took them and left the room. She was back before he had a chance to regulate his heartbeat, wearing the clean boxers and T-shirt he'd handed her.

Holy cow! The thin knit shirt might as well have been made out of cobwebs, the way it revealed every single one of her mouth-watering curves. He nearly choked when his tongue got stuck to the roof of his mouth.

Twin temptations pushed the TEXAS RACEWAY lettering on the shirt front right out there for God and everybody to see. Seeing those boxers of his barely hanging on to the sweet roundness of her hips shot his heart rate straight to the moon. *For cryin' out loud, Walker. What were you thinking? You should've given her a pair of old sweats or something.*

If the room had seemed small before, he was damn certain the sides were closing in on him now. Catching his breath was turning into a major project. Help!

Her presence was everywhere, surrounding him with clouds of warm apple-blossom fragrance. He fought with the images playing leap-frog in his mind. Images that had no business being there at all. Images that were going to get him in a heap of trouble if he didn't watch out. Ooooh, yeah!

He tried not to ogle her tantalizing figure as he folded back the faded quilt on his bed. He couldn't envision Faith becoming a mother. In his mind, she was still that slightly rebellious teenager always landing in some kind of scrape. Always expecting him to rescue her.

Maybe if her belly'd been round like a watermelon, he wouldn't have had so much trouble with the erotic visions lurking in the corners of his mind. *Concentrate, Walker.* He flipped the pillows over, checked their cases and tried to act cool, which he definitely was not.

His tongue finally came unglued from the roof of his mouth and felt measurably normal now. "I think you'll be comfortable here," he said, proving that feeling right.

When he turned around, she was right there, only inches away, with a smile on her face so heart-shatteringly sweet, his whole body went on Red Alert. He stepped back, bumped into the side of the bed and realized retreat was impossible. The B-E-D. Damn.

"You are my very best friend, Buddy Lee."

She touched his hand, and a spear of fire shot right up his arm. Sweet words, but not exactly the ones he'd ever expected to hear on the eve of his wedding. Let's face it, he'd never expected to even have a wedding, let alone the *eve* of one. Right now, his thoughts were so tangled he couldn't put a sentence together. He never expected Faith to be climbing into his bed, either. Even if he wasn't going to share it with her. The whole scenario was unreal. Fantasy time. Imagination overload.

Had to be a full moon or something equally disrupting, to cause such an uproar in his life.

"It'll be all right, Faith." *Oh sure, Walker, like you know.* He wanted to reassure her somehow. Needed to tell her he would take care of everything. But other than wanting to cause Royce some serious bodily harm, he didn't know what exactly it was he was supposed to take care of.

Then her bottom lip trembled, and he came undone for want of a taste of that luscious mouth. For the need to touch her, to protect her. To love her.

He all but leaped around her, setting her aside and rushing for the door. "Uh, just yell if you need anything."

In his haste to escape before he lost all good sense, he smacked his shin against the doorframe. He bit back an oath and welcomed the needles of pain in his leg. They diverted his attention from the other pain—the one carving holes in his heart.

Later, lying motionless on the lumpy sofa, he sorted through his thoughts. Or tried to. Faith was in the next room, his room, tucked cozily between his sheets and wearing nothing more than a pair of his dark blue boxers and his Texas Raceway T-shirt. What kept his jaw in a teeth-grinding clinch was his envy of those sheets, of his shirt. And, dammit, he was waaaay jealous of his boxers right then. How pathetic was that?

He counted the cracks in the ceiling where the paint peeled in the corners. Tried visualizing the remaining restoration work needed on his Mustang, locked safely away at the shop. But that was a bad idea because it stirred up fantasies of Faith and him tangled in a heated, back seat body lock.

What was he getting himself into? Marrying Faith strictly as an act of friendship, especially knowing that Royce had been her lover, was about to become the challenge of his lifetime. Even though she'd hinted at a less than satisfactory experience with Royce, the fact was, *it* had happened. And didn't that just open up a whole slew of mental images vivid enough to win an Oscar?

Aw, man, at this rate his eyes were never going to shut. He shot off the couch and stomped down the hall. He really hated cold showers.

Faith crawled into the unfamiliar bed, wrapped her arms around the extra pillow and pulled it close to her chest. A whiff of something warm, comforting, and extremely male reminded her of Buddy Lee. She sank further down into his scent, snugging the sheet over her body like a reassuring caress.

Secure. That's how he made her feel. Always had. She'd never even hesitated about running to him for help tonight. Reflecting on the circumstances now, she realized there wasn't anyone else she could turn to. Not even her family. She'd made a mess of things again and expected him to make it better. Old habits die hard, but this time, she'd make it up to him. She only needed to be married long enough to convince her family and Royce that the baby was Buddy Lee's. She wouldn't hold him to a lifetime commitment. That wouldn't be fair.

She sighed and closed her eyes. Maybe if she concentrated real hard, the awful events of the past few weeks would slip into the realm of dark oblivion and she'd be able to sleep. Morning was soon enough to face whatever lay ahead. *Buddy Lee, what on Earth have I gotten us into now?*

Just then, the thud of bare feet tromping down the hall broke through her half-sleep. The sound couldn't have been any louder if Buddy Lee had been wearing boots. Lying perfectly still, she listened as he marched toward the bathroom. Was he having trouble sleeping, too? The rumble of the water pipes and the sound of the shower splattering against the cubicle wall said "Yes."

She slipped out of bed and tiptoed to the window. Nothing moved on the quiet street except for a stray yellow cat darting under the porch of the house across the way.

Liberty never had been much of a town for nightlife. How could it be, with only a population of fifteen-hundred, give or take a few, depending on the day and who'd gone fishing?

She smiled, recalling her teenage goal to remedy Liberty's simple lifestyle by providing a few unorthodox and often disorderly events for the community's enjoyment. Buddy Lee had been relentless in his own goal to keep her from achieving her objective and save her from her daddy's wrath. She'd accused him of being a stick-in-the-mud on more than one occasion, but he'd remained her constant defender. Why he'd put up with her shenanigans back then puzzled her, but she'd accepted it without looking for reasons. Had she really been that shallow?

The unwavering support he offered her now simply reinforced her fondness for him. If she could choose a big brother, she'd pick one exactly like Buddy Lee. She'd be sure to make a point of telling him how much she treasured his friendship.

Water pipes banged again. Unidentifiable bumps and squeaks joined the sound. But it was the total silence that sent her scurrying back to bed. Her heart did a little dance when heavy footsteps paused in front of her door.

He thought he'd heard her moving around in there. That was the only reason he'd stopped in front of the bedroom door and listened. Yeah, right. And when he convinced himself of that, he'd work on believing Lionel Morgan was gonna welcome him as a son-in-law, too. Uh-huh. He could almost hear the 'gators belly-laughing.

What would it matter if he just peeked in to see if she was asleep? Wouldn't make any difference at all, unless she heard him. Then he'd have to explain why he was lurking outside her door. He'd already said "good-night."

Dammit, he didn't want to admit that the idea of being a married man and a daddy-to-be all in the space of a few hours had him scared spitless. Married, for cryin' out loud. To Faith! Just the thought of sharing space with her on a permanent basis had his insides twisted in a knot.

He wiped sweaty palms across his clean T-shirt and felt a flush sneak up his neck to warm his face. *So much for the cold shower.* Cautiously, he nudged the door open a crack and leaned forward just far enough to see into the room.

Shadow puppets created by the streetlight danced across the wall. His gaze tracked them to the bed and the phantom-like outline of Faith sitting there. Watching him. Aw, shoot.

"Hey, Faith," he whispered, for lack of a better comment. In spite of all the childish experiences they'd shared years ago, seeing a grown-up Faith in his bed tonight gave a whole new interpretation of the word *friendship.*

"Hey, Buddy Lee," came her soft response.

He couldn't see her face clearly, but he was certain he heard a smile in her voice. He took one step inside the room. Shoved his hands in his jeans pockets. Exhaled when he realized he'd been holding his breath.

"You couldn't sleep, either?" Another step toward the bed brought him close enough to see her face illuminated by the silvery light. Her burnished curls shone bright as a new penny, and her green eyes sparkled with tiny lights. That lush mouth curved up in a familiar smile, and his good intentions had a meltdown.

"Huh-uh. Too wound up, I guess." She scooted over, patting a place on the bed next to her. "Come sit by me. If we can't sleep, we might as well talk about tomorrow's plan of action. I mean, besides getting married and all."

Sitting down on that bed next to her was the last thing he ought to be doing. Still, she was right about needing to make plans for tomorrow. Hell, he didn't have a clue how to go about getting married. Especially the "and all" stuff.

"There's a waiting period, isn't there? And what about the license you and Royce already have?"

"Royce doesn't have it, I do. When we applied in Allen County, the clerk told us the license would expire if we didn't use it within thirty days, so there shouldn't be a problem. You and I will apply in Granite City. That's in Newcomb County. Don't worry, I've got it figured out."

That didn't surprise him, since she'd already been through the process with Royce-the-Jackass. Besides, when had Faith ever *not* had her plans organized. Even when she was fixin' to pull some stupid stunt as a kid, she'd had a plan. She always had a plan.

So, how could she have forgotten to plan for this baby? That just wasn't like her. And how the heck was he supposed to deal with a hot-tempered ex-fiancé who, when he found out what they'd done, would probably like nothing better than to see Buddy Lee swinging from the nearest tree? Or shot and field-dressed.

He sat next to her anyway. What the heck. There'd be plenty of time to deal with Royce later. Besides, he was making a few plans of his own about that. "So what's your plan?"

Faith smoothed out the sheet she pulled over her legs and folded her hands in her lap. "I thought we could leave for Granite City early, right after breakfast," she said, all details and business now. "We'll get the license tomorrow, get married Friday, then tell Daddy afterwards."

Tell Daddy. Now that was something to look forward to. Right up there with root canals and head lice.

"But I'll have to stay here for now. My parents don't expect me in town until time for the rehearsal Friday night."

"Here? Right now?" Buddy Lee's world was dangerously close to becoming an impossible dream. Letting Faith share his home before the wedding wasn't in the game plan he expected. He figured he'd have three days of getting used to the idea of marrying Faith before they actually lived together.

"What about Royce?" He would've preferred to meet that man privately. He didn't want an audience when he turned the jerk into a soprano-singing eunuch.

"Oh, I don't ever want to see him again. Daddy can tell him." When she shuddered, Buddy Lee slid his arm around her shoulders.

"Yeah, okay. So, after we tell your folks, then what?" Seemed like he ought to be having a say here, but he could wait until later to sort out his thoughts. Right now, his brain buzzed like a hive full of confused worker bees whose queen was out of control.

"I suppose it depends on their reaction, but I can promise you, Daddy will shout up a storm and Mama will disappear into her bedroom, like she always does in a crisis." Faith turned toward Buddy Lee and scootched her hips closer, curling her legs against him and leaning back against the headboard. "We haven't talked about where we'll live after we're married, you know."

Well, hoo-ha! Who's had time? he wanted to ask, but didn't. His heart rate was about as rapid as it could get before it stopped completely, so he took a deep breath to settle it. He oughta move. His skin was heating up where Faith's legs pushed against him from under the sheet. But he stayed right there.

"I can't just up and leave here, Faith. I've got a business to run." And money to make, for cryin' out loud. "If you tell me what you need, I'll fix up that little room in back for a nursery." A sobering thought, having a baby's nursery in his house. But, he'd do whatever he had to...for Faith.

The area he spoke of was actually a tiny combination laundry room and breezeway connecting the house and garage, but since he didn't own any laundry appliances, the room stored his extra tools and auto parts. Cluttered, but easily cleaned when the time came. How much space did a baby need, anyway?

She looked at him dreamily. "Imagine, Buddy Lee. A real baby. The only good thing about this whole mess. And it'll be yours...mine...uh, well, you know what I mean."

She yawned and nestled her head against his chest. *So much for serious discussions.* Her soft, even breathing mingled provocatively with the not-so-even thud of his own heartbeat. He settled her more comfortably into the crook of his arm and figured he'd stay where he was for a little longer. Only to make sure she was sound asleep. Then he'd move back to the safety of his lumpy sofa.

When he left her an hour later, he was no closer to having any answers than he had been earlier.

And he didn't have any the next day, either, when they headed for Granite City to get a piece of paper that would tie them together legally for however long Faith wanted. All he had to do was make it through the next three days without the damned alligators catching him.

When Friday finally rolled around, Buddy Lee swore every 'gator in Louisiana had come across the state line looking for him.

Chapter Three

"**D**early beloved, we are gathered here ..."

The minister's voice droned on in a tedious monotone that made it easy for Buddy Lee's own thoughts to wander.

Late afternoon shadows played against the walls of the living room in the modestly-furnished parsonage. Even with Faith's detailed plans, the necessary arrangements for their wedding had taken longer to complete than they had expected.

Now they stood in front of a very young minister who'd been kind enough to agree to perform the ceremony in his home. The minister's wife stood as witness to the vows they were about to take, along with a hastily recruited neighbor named Otis something-or-other. Faith had objected to using the services of a Justice of the Peace, and since she'd given up her fancy wedding, Buddy Lee didn't argue with her.

He still wasn't certain how Faith had managed to find the reverend. How many other surprises was she going to spring on him? No doubt, more than he was prepared for.

He stared, ashamed, at the meager bunch of flowers clutched in her hands. Tied with narrow, white satin ribbon, they were colorful but common as roadside wildflowers. Like him. She deserved better. He'd had to swallow his pride when she paid for the expense of the license and ceremony. That really stuck in his craw. He was short of cash, as usual.

That morning, he'd barely had time to do more than flip the "Closed" sign on his shop window and get his one-and-only good pair of pants on before Faith started pulling him out the door. Since the Texas Truckin' T-shirt he usually wore didn't seem appropriate, he hoped his plaid shirt was okay. At least, it was clean.

He stifled a yawn. The past two nights he'd sprawled on the sofa-from-Hell, tossing restlessly until dawn streaked the sky. Thinking. Wondering what the future held and trying to convince himself it didn't matter if Faith wasn't marrying him for love. He was pretty sure he had enough for them both. He couldn't quite decide how he felt about being a daddy yet, but he would soon. Well, as soon as he figured out what a good father really was. What if he turned out like his old man? It wasn't like Boyd Walker had been a role model of decency. Neither was Faith's daddy, for that matter. Come to think of it, he and the woman about to become his wife had both missed out on that score.

The minister's wife coughed politely, and Buddy Lee forced his attention back to the ceremony and Faith, sweet Faith.

The last thirty dollars stuffed in his wallet for his Mustang fund had gone to buy the simple bouquet she had chosen. The florist's raised eyebrows and *tsk-tsks* had embarrassed him something awful, but Faith had acted like it was the most elegant arrangement in the shop. When she'd picked out a tiny yellow rosebud and pinned it on his collar, his face had burned flash-fire hot, along with other portions of his anatomy. Did roses really go with plaid shirts?

He shifted his gaze from the plain bouquet to Faith's glowing face. His heart was smiling. He could feel it, even though marrying her was the last thing he ever thought would happen in his lifetime. Yep, his ol' ticker was grinning with every excited thump it made, and he couldn't help feeling like the luckiest person alive. Now, if that luck would just hold out when they told her daddy what they'd gone and done.

Just then, a corner of Faith's mouth curved upwards. She tilted her face, and Buddy Lee recognized the slow smile she used to give him when they were kids. The same one that had captured his heart and held it all these years.

A wave of tenderness swept through him and his eyes grew damp. Just allergies, he thought, because Buddy Lee Walker never cried.

As small and fragile as she was, Faith had always been bigger than life to him. Maybe it was because she'd always treated him as an equal, even though she came from the privileged side of town and his home had been a tiny, three-room tract-house. She never referred to him as *Boyd's boy*, either, like the rest of the town was inclined to do.

He remembered when she'd graduated from the University of Texas with a degree in social services or something like that. He'd been the only one in town who wasn't surprised when she moved away from home. Everyone else expected her to stay in Liberty, get married and settle down. Some folks said her daddy blew a gasket and threatened to cut off her money if she moved. The big shocker came when she told him to go ahead and do it. That sent her mama to bed for a week. Last he'd heard, Faith was working in Granite City for some kind of community service organization. 'Course, she'd always been a nurturer and champion of the less fortunate. Shoot, hadn't she befriended him—white trash to the highest power?

"Do you, Buddy Lee Walker, take Faith Nicole Morgan..."

The monotone voice was a little stronger and firmer now, and Buddy Lee figured he'd best pay attention to this part.

Faith stood close enough for him to breathe in the scent of her shampoo—the familiar sweet fragrance that tangled his senses and messed with his mind. She leaned against him, her arm touching his in a closeness that shattered what was left of his composure. The warmth of her touch heated his arm right through his shirtsleeve, and his instant arousal embarrassed him. Then she nudged him in the ribs, hard, and that took care of that.

The minister cleared his throat. Faith nudged him again.

Buddy Lee squared his shoulders and flashed a wide smile. "I do."

"Do you, Faith Nicole Morgan, take Buddy Lee Walker..."

Faith looked at the man standing beside her and knew she was making the right decision.

She'd run straight into Buddy Lee's arms Monday night, looking for safety but finding a great deal more. The shock of unexpected longing that swept through her still held her in awe. She hadn't known she was capable of such intense feelings. Certainly hadn't expected to experience them with Buddy Lee. She wasn't quite certain how to deal with them, either.

During her college years, she'd had casual, non-committal dates. None caused any great sexual thrill or spurred any deep need to explore them further. She'd met Royce when he joined the staff of her daddy's bank.

Impressed by the new employee, Lionel Morgan was soon grooming Royce for promotion and introducing him to his daughter.

Instantly attracted to Royce's good looks and likeable personality, Faith was flattered by his amorous attentions and easily persuaded to accept his proposal. She'd been so sure what she felt was love. But she'd been wrong. The sensations she'd experienced then were lukewarm compared to the heat stirring inside her now. Nothing could have surprised her more than the flash of raw passion Buddy Lee's touch had created.

Remembering how frightened she'd been of Royce, she let her gaze rest on Buddy Lee's stalwart features and absorbed his quiet strength. He made her feel so warm and secure, not afraid. Funny, they'd been good friends as kids, nothing more. He'd been her protector and defender, taking the blame for her silly pranks when she should've owned up to them. She'd thought it hilarious at the time. Then their lives had taken different paths. She'd never expected him to be more than a casual friend. And now, here they were, getting married. She thought about the baby she carried. Life was good at throwing curves.

She squeezed his hand and he squeezed hers back in a way that warmed her all over. He really was her dearest friend. That was all these feelings of hers could possibly mean.

"...until death parts you from this union?"

"Of course, I do," came Faith's confident answer.

Buddy Lee grinned at her then and reached into his pocket. When he pulled out his big, heavy class ring and put it on her finger, she had to make a fist to keep it from sliding off, but she didn't care. Thanks to him, she'd never have to become Mrs. Royce Webb. And her baby would be safe.

"You may kiss your bride." The minister nodded to Buddy Lee with a wide smile.

Buddy Lee didn't move.

After only a second's hesitation, Faith nudged him. She lifted her face to her new husband and felt a little zip of electricity race beneath the surface of her skin.

Then the zip exploded into a full-fledged shock as he angled his head and touched his lips to hers.

At precisely three minutes after two, Buddy Lee swung his truck into the arc of the circular drive gracing the front of the Morgan mansion and cut the engine. He stared long and hard at the imposing two-story Victorian structure belonging to his wife's parents. The unsuspecting pair inside had no clue they'd just become his in-laws. *This oughta' be a real show-stopper.*

Sweat popped out on his upper lip, even though the truck's air-conditioning kept the interior at a cool seventy-two degrees. He took a couple of deep breaths to still his jangled nerves. Didn't help much.

Okay, if he survived the upcoming confrontation with Faith's parents, he figured he could pretty well survive anything. Right now, with his heart kabooming and his pulse jumping, he doubted his survival skills could help him fight his way out of a Piggly-Wiggly shopping bag. He swallowed around the prickly lump in his throat and snuck a glance at Faith.

She sat next to him, stiff as a fence post and just as silent, not like herself at all, which bothered him some. Was she thinking about the kiss? He sure as hell was. He should have just given her a little peck on the cheek, friendly like. After all, they hadn't agreed to anything more. He'd kept the kiss chaste...almost. God, he'd wanted to kiss her thoroughly and taste her sweetness. It had taken every bit of his wavering self-control not to give in.

He hadn't missed the way she'd been keeping her hands locked together on the drive over, or the way she occasionally rubbed the rough surface of the heavy gold ring on her third finger, left hand. Well, he'd already apologized for the substitute wedding ring. He wasn't going to apologize for the kiss, dammit.

He reached for the door handle, slid out. *Here goes nothing.* As he rounded the front of the pickup to open Faith's door, his heart started bouncing back and forth between his throat and the pit of his stomach like it was lost. He offered a shaky hand to his wife. *His wife?* Oh, man, what had they done?

"Come on, Buddy Lee." With her hand tucked in his, Faith approached the front door with only minor twitches in her pulse. She wasn't afraid of her daddy. Four and a half years at the university had helped her realize that she did, indeed, have a backbone and not just a talent for being irresponsible. Not that her current dilemma was any proof of that. She'd gotten herself into a fine mess this time, dragging Buddy Lee along with her.

Defying her daddy wasn't the only bad thing she'd done, either. She'd made her best friend an accomplice to the lie she was about to tell her family. And probably put him in danger, if Royce ever discovered the truth. Or if the truth was ever discovered about Royce. That was what frightened her. What *was* the truth about Royce? How could she have been so wrong?

Well, keeping the two men apart, no matter what, was imperative. She sighed. How could she have ever believed she was in love with Royce Webb? Especially after the strangely exciting way Buddy Lee's single kiss had made her toes curl.

Buddy Lee barely had time to punch the doorbell before the door swung open and Lionel Morgan loomed in front of them, his florid face distorted in a scowl.

"Where have you been, girl?" He reached out and grabbed at his daughter's arm. His eyes widened in surprise when she shrugged free and met his glare with a flash of boldness, calmly smoothing her sleeve where her father's hand had twisted it.

"Hello, Daddy. You remember Buddy Lee Walker, don't you? We'd like to come in and talk to you and Mama." There was no mistaking the saccharine sweetness of her words or the strength behind them.

Lionel looked Buddy Lee up and down. "Boyd's boy, aren't you?" His voice was as rough as his face was ugly.

Buddy Lee ground his teeth, stretching his lips into a tight smile. The man knew damned well who he was. He'd been the one to approve the loan for the auto shop. But if Faith insisted on playing the sugar-sweet part, so would he. For a while, anyway.

"Some folks call me that, yessir." He stuck out his hand, mentally daring Lionel to shake it. When the older man ignored the gesture, Buddy Lee shoved his hand back in his pocket with an unconcerned shrug and a mental, not-so-nice suggestion for the banker.

Faith moved closer to her new husband, their sides touching. "We need to talk to you now, Daddy." Her voice grew stronger, and Buddy Lee detected a stiffening in her spine, so he squared his shoulders. He slid a protective arm around his wife, damned proud of how she managed to keep her cool.

"What you need to do is get yourself upstairs, young lady," Lionel roared. "Your mama's been sick with worry. You were supposed to be here this morning. Did you forget the rehearsal is at five o'clock? And you," Faith's daddy pinned a steely glare on Buddy Lee, "you get the hell off my property before I have you arrested for...for..." The more he sputtered, the redder his face got.

"I didn't forget anything, Daddy. And don't threaten my husband." Faith's quiet words cut through her father's angry shouts, instantly silencing him.

The prickly lump that had been sitting in Buddy Lee's throat all morning finally expanded to choking proportions. All hell was about to break loose, just as he'd expected, and he and Faith were standing smack dab in the line of fire. The notion to grab his wife and run whizzed through his brain for a nanosecond right before his good sense kicked in.

Then he felt Faith's warm hand on his arm and knew he wasn't going anywhere at all. Not if this precious woman needed him to protect and support her, or whatever in the wide world she wanted from him. He was her man now, for better or worse. That was the vow he'd made in front of the preacher, and he aimed to keep it, even though he feared the *worse* was coming sooner than the *better*. Lionel Morgan looked like he was fixin' to explode.

"You're *what*?" Morgan's words thundered through the air like a tent-revival evangelist's and Buddy Lee swore he felt the ground shake.

He found Faith's hand and gripped it tight. When she squeezed back and gave him that sweet smile again, his off-kilter world righted itself.

"That's right, Mr. Morgan, sir. Faith and I are married. That's what we came to tell you." It was hard to talk with a mouth drier than chalk, but Buddy Lee figured he'd managed well enough for the man to understand what he'd said.

"Beryl! Beryl, come down here!" The roar Lionel emitted when he called his wife's name was loud enough to wake the residents of the local cemetery two miles outside of town.

While they waited in the doorway, Buddy Lee stole a glance past the outraged man on the chance he might spot any shotguns close by. Better to know what odds he was facing, in case he and Faith had to make a quick exit off the porch. Never hurt to be prepared.

Beryl Morgan glided down the staircase and took her place next to her husband. Clad in a diaphanous robe of pale yellow, the frail woman was nearly invisible in the shadow of her portly spouse. Pale skin, pale hair. To Buddy Lee's way of thinking, she looked downright sickly.

"What on earth is the matter, Lionel?" Beryl's voice was as frail as her stature. Her hands fluttered at her throat. She stared blankly at her daughter. "Why, hello, dear. Why are you standing in the door?"

Lionel ignored his wife and scowled at the couple. "You two get in here and do some explaining. And it had better be damn good." He turned and stomped down the hall.

Faith brushed her mother's cheek with a kiss. "Let's go in, Mama, and we'll tell you all about it."

As Beryl followed her husband down the wide hall, Faith tugged on Buddy Lee's hand. "C'mon," she urged. "We have to tell them. Just remember, let me do the explaining. All you have to do is agree with whatever I say, okay?"

That was the same directive she'd given him too many times before. He nodded, but a creepy feeling of *déjà vu* crawled up his spine. The way his mouth dried up and his tongue tied itself in a knot, he couldn't have talked much anyhow.

He did wonder, though, why Faith was suddenly so calm and determined, when last night she'd come to him in hysterics over Royce's rough and secretive actions. Had getting married made that much of a change in her? He didn't claim to be a math whiz, but something here wasn't adding up. He wasn't quite sure what to make of the whole thing.

Lionel motioned to a quartet of white wicker chairs fitted with plump, yellow and blue print cushions. Buddy Lee waited until everyone else was seated before taking the chair next to Faith. He made a quick visual inspection of his surroundings.

The room was nearly the size of his entire house. Light and airy, it afforded a spectacular view of the colorful gardens surrounding a sparkling swimming pool. A perfect spot for an intimate chat. Or a loud confrontation. He had already figured out which one this was likely to be. Oh, yeah. He wiped his sweaty palms on his denim-clad legs.

"Daddy. Mama. Like we explained, Buddy Lee and I got married this afternoon."

Buddy Lee noticed Faith visibly holding her breath, so maybe she wasn't so confident, after all. He wasn't sure if he felt better or worse, but when Lionel jumped up and grabbed him by the shirt front, *worse* pretty well covered it.

Lionel pushed his face right up next to his. "Impossible! She's marrying Royce tomorrow."

He stood close enough for him to get a real good whiff of the man's strong whiskey breath, but Buddy Lee stood his ground. "No sir, she's not."

Morgan made a move, ready to swing a fist, but Faith grabbed his arm. "Stop it, Daddy! You're making Mama have a fainting spell."

She rushed to the built-in bar across the room and poured a glass of water for her mother. "Here, Mama, drink this. You'll feel better in a minute."

Lionel waved aside his daughter's protest. "Never mind her. She faints at the drop of a hat." He turned to his wife. "Beryl, pay attention. Didn't you hear what our daughter just said? She's gone and married Boyd Walker's boy when she's supposed to be marrying Royce tomorrow. Faint about that if you have to faint about something."

He let go of Buddy Lee and pushed him back into the chair. "You'd better have a damn good reason for this, boy. I ought to haul your no-account carcass right over to the county jail."

"You're not hauling anybody anywhere, Daddy," Faith said before Buddy Lee had a chance to put his Adam's apple back where it belonged. "We're married and having a baby. You'll just have to cancel the wedding arrangements."

Beryl slumped to the floor in a dead faint, just as Lionel's fist shot out like a well-aimed missile. Buddy Lee ducked a second too late and wound up with a humdinger of a bloody nose, courtesy of his brand new father-in-law.

Well, hell.

Faith's daddy started shouting about the cost of canceling the wedding and threatening to have Buddy Lee arrested. Her mama finally came to, flitting around and bemoaning the fact that the family's good name and reputation were going to be ruined. The two were so busy blaming each other for not keeping their daughter under control, they didn't even notice when the couple slipped out of the house and drove away. Buddy Lee drove with one hand on the steering wheel, the other holding his handkerchief on his nose.

By the time they left Liberty's city limits, he'd already made a mess of his handkerchief. Forty-five minutes later, they were sitting in the Cactus Pear Bar and Grill on the outskirts of Granite City, far enough away to feel safe. At least, for the time being.

Faith held a wet paper napkin to her husband's swollen nose. "I'm so sorry, Buddy Lee," she said, with a hitch in her soft voice. "I never meant for you to get hurt."

"'S'okay," Buddy Lee mumbled, wondering if his nose looked as big as it felt. Lionel Morgan's fist had come out of nowhere, and he hadn't had a chance to duck. The old man packed quite a punch, too. Buddy Lee would've swung back if it had been anyone but Faith's daddy. Shoot, he wasn't *that* dumb. Besides, he'd been sitting down at the time and too surprised to react.

The waitress brought two colas, a glass of ice cubes and a clean bar towel. Faith thanked her and wrapped the cloth around three of the cubes.

"Hold this on your nose. It will help the swelling go down."

"Mm-hmm." Buddy Lee stuck the freezing bundle on his throbbing face. He didn't feel any better, but he appreciated Faith's effort. She was trying to make the best of things but, truth was, he felt about as useful as hip pockets on a hog right then. Some husband he was turning out to be. He was supposed to be taking care of her.

He shifted the ice pack over so he could talk. "Maybe we'd better decide what we're gonna' do next. You think your daddy'll come after us?" Sobering as that thought was, Buddy Lee wasn't about to let the Morgans make Faith's life any more miserable. It was up to him to look after her now. But a pregnant bride was a whole new experience. He desperately needed a how-to book for situations like this because he didn't have a clue where to begin.

"It's not Daddy I'm worried about." Faith glanced toward the tavern door. "It's Royce. I'm not sure what he'll do. He isn't the man I thought he was, Buddy Lee. All these months, he had me fooled." She shuddered. "Until Monday night. How could I have been so wrong?"

Buddy Lee reached across the table and folded her hand in his. "Don't worry, Faith. There's nothing he can do now. We're married. It's a done deal."

She sighed and squeezed his hand. "You are so good to me, Buddy Lee. Just like when we were kids."

Yeah, well, they weren't kids anymore and he was pretty sure his feelings for Faith weren't child-like in any way, shape or form. Nope, not at all. And he didn't know how in heck he was going to handle *that*.

He studied their entwined hands resting on the scarred tabletop and a silly grin kicked up the corners of his mouth. For a minute, he had a goofy urge to pull out his pocketknife and carve their initials next to all the others that had been embedded there over the past decade or so. Talk about juvenile. *Get a grip, Walker.*

"You know, we should be heading back home," he said, after they had finished their drinks. He'd made an effort to take a couple of sips of his soda, but his puffed-up lip made him dribble like a baby, so he set it aside. "You should rest after this long day, shouldn't you, Faith? I mean, in your condition and all. For the baby."

Buddy Lee's stammered sincerity warmed Faith's heart. He really was concerned about her, and she felt awful about this whole mess. This wasn't what she'd planned, but she wasn't surprised. Daddy could be mean when he was upset. And she'd certainly upset him by marrying Buddy Lee. She hadn't given much thought as to where home was going to be. There were two weeks left on her apartment lease, but that was empty except for the usual appliances that came with it. Still, Buddy Lee's house would be the first place her parents would look. And Royce. They couldn't forget about him. There was something sinister and dangerous about his threats that really frightened her. Buddy Lee couldn't be expected to commute from Granite City to his shop in Liberty, either. That was nearly forty miles one way. Why hadn't she thought of that before? *Dummy. You really screwed up this time.*

"I, uh, maybe we'd better stay in a motel, just for tonight." She didn't want to go back to Liberty tonight, now that they'd announced their marriage. She was terrified of what might happen after Daddy broke the news to Royce.

"A...motel?" Buddy Lee stared, wide-eyed.

"Don't worry, I've got my credit card with me," she hurried to assure him. Finances were another topic they needed to discuss, too. She didn't want to be a burden to him. She had her own money. They'd work out something. Right after they found a motel with a vacancy.

The motel attached to the Cactus Pear Bar and Grill wasn't the fanciest establishment in the area, but it was far enough away from Liberty for Faith to feel sure her daddy wouldn't be bothering them.

She listened, wide-eyed, as the desk clerk explained there were no vacancies. How could that be when the place didn't even deserve a three-star rating?

"Big convention in town this weekend," the clerk said. "Most everything is filled right up. Sorry, folks."

Buddy Lee turned to Faith. "Got any other ideas?"

She hesitated. "My place isn't too far from here, but there's no bed. Or any other furniture," she quickly added, not wanting to give the impression she was only thinking about their sleeping arrangements, although she was. "We'd have to sleep on the floor." Their only other option was to return to Buddy Lee's house, and she was afraid of what might happen if Royce decided to show up there. Besides, it was late and they hadn't had any dinner. "We could pick up a pizza on the way."

The way his stomach was growling, he'd have agreed to most anything edible, even though pizza was way down on his list of likeables. Chicken-fried steak, now that was a man's meal.

"Sounds like a plan," he said, putting as much enthusiasm in his voice as he could muster. Then he remembered something that made him smile from the inside out. "And don't worry about a bed. I always carry a sleeping bag in the truck."

Chapter Four

The spicy aroma of thick-crusted pizza with extra cheese, no onions, filled the empty apartment with a cozy warmth that almost had Buddy Lee relaxing. Almost.

His wife—*man, I love the sound of that word*—sat cross-legged on the old red sleeping bag he'd spread out over the carpeted floor, licking pizza sauce from her lips the way a contented cat licks cream from its whiskers. He watched, mesmerized, as the tip of her tongue slid out and slowly circled her mouth. His nervous system was anything but relaxed. Wired was more like it. A rocket ready to launch. Didn't matter, though. He'd have to keep those twinges of longing to himself. *Just friends, Walker. Remember that.*

"Mmmm, I love pizza, don't you?" She smiled and reached for another slice. "I'm sorry this turned out to be such a horrible day." She touched his arm, suddenly full of sympathy. "Does your nose still hurt?"

"No, not a bit." *Hell, yes.* He helped himself to more pizza. It hurt to chew, but he was too hungry to care. And he sure wasn't going to admit to a little bit of pain. Not on your life. He was supposed to be the rescuer here.

She passed him a bottle of water. He took it and wished for a cold beer. And pain pills. And all the things he knew could never be.

"This is absolutely the worst predicament I've ever put us in, isn't it?" Faith's voice was soft, but he heard her loud and clear.

They were stretched out side by side on the sleeping bag, Buddy Lee struggling to put more space between his rigid body and Faith's soft, tempting one. This was a whole lot different than sleeping on the sofa while she'd been occupying his bed. At least then, there'd been the bedroom wall between them. He tried not to think about how close they were now.

The swirled pattern of the apartment's Berber carpet had already imprinted itself in his shoulder, right next to the teeth marks from the bag's zippered edge. Careful not to breach the six or so inches separating them, he shifted to find a more comfortable position. There was none. If he moved his arm forward, he'd touch the softness of her shoulder. If he moved his leg to straighten it, he'd brush against the smooth length of hers. If he didn't make either of those moves, he'd likely die of frustration. He wanted to touch her and knew he shouldn't. Their marriage was just on paper.

Rolling over on his side, he propped himself up on one elbow to gaze down at her. With his knuckles, he gently coaxed her face toward his. He wanted to see her eyes when they spoke. Needed to search for answers in their depths—to have her look at him with the same longing that curled inside his gut. Wanted to watch those soft lips curve into a smile. Man, he was turning to mush. Correction. Not all parts of his anatomy. Nope, certain parts were painfully hard.

"Buddy Lee, did you hear what I said?"

"Hmmm?" Her eyes were the clearest, richest green he'd ever seen. Her mouth was full, ripe, and he wanted ....

Her forefinger poked at his chest. "You're not even listening, are you?"

With her face so close and her mouth so lush and inviting, did she really expect him to make conversation, for cryin' out loud?

"Sorry," he mumbled, his gaze never straying from her mouth.

She frowned, and he resented being distracted from the totally enticing images floating around in his mind.

"Honestly, Buddy Lee, aren't you the least bit upset? I mean, this time I really got us in deep." She trailed her hand down the long, taut muscle of his forearm until her fingers met his. Stayed there.

He made a fist around her hand, but kept staring at her mouth. Couldn't tear his gaze away. He should say something, but no words came out. All he wanted was to capture a taste of her lips. Yeah, his mouth on hers. Her mouth on....

With a sudden, painful return to reality, he rocketed off the sleeping bag. "Upset? Upset? Hell, yes, I'm upset." She didn't know the half of it. Sweet mercy, he needed to find a tub full of ice and jump in. Diving in head first would be even better. Why had he ever thought he could be married to Faith without touching her? He was no saint. Didn't want to be.

He paced the room, careful to keep his back to her. When his body relaxed so he could finally turn around, she was watching him through eyes wide and damp. Aw, shoot, now he'd made her cry.

"Darlin', don't do that," he said, and hurried to kneel beside her. "I shouldn't have yelled, you being pregnant and all. I'm sorry." He rubbed her hands between his. "Can I get you something? Water?" He glanced around the bare room. "More pizza?"

"I really believe you're more naive than I am, Buddy Lee." She wiped the back of her hand across her eyes. "Don't you know pregnant women cry most of the time? And for no apparent reason?"

"Now, how would I know anything about that?" Was he in for eight more months of her tears?

"Isn't this silly? Here I am, pregnant by a man I loathe, but married to my best friend who's agreed to give my child his name, and I'm the one being a crybaby. I should be thanking you, not bawling all over you."

She sniffled and Buddy Lee automatically reached for his handkerchief, but he'd forgotten he'd used it on his battered nose, so he snagged a paper napkin from the stack next to the pizza box instead.

He gave her the napkin. "Let's start over, okay?"

Faith blinked rapidly several times, then dabbed at her weepy eyes.

"You're absolutely right. We need to plan our strategy. Obviously we can't live here." She waved her hand at the empty room. "Living with Daddy and Mama is out, too."

Damn straight. Buddy Lee nearly laughed out loud at that astute observation He kept quiet because he'd just discovered that as long as Faith stayed busy making plans, she forgot to cry. And if that's what it took to make her happy, he was willing to put up with a truck load of plan-making. He reckoned that before long there'd be a baby to take over the crying business when Faith finished with her part. He wasn't sure just how that was going to work out.

A reckless thought about needing a bigger house darted across his confused mind. Just as swiftly, he rejected it.

Shoot, he could barely afford the one he had, even if it was small. At least he owned it free and clear after years of scrimping and saving, so old man Morgan's bank couldn't put a claim on it. The house was the only thing his no-account daddy never got his hands on.

"Where do you want to live, darlin'?" Might as well ask, but the way he had it figured, there was only one answer to that. His place or no place. He had a business to run and he sure couldn't do it from Granite City.

Faith gave him a thoughtful appraisal, then said, "I guess we'll have to live in your house. I'll never go back to the other one. I don't care how much Daddy paid for it."

"What about your job?"

"I'll keep it for a while. I can commute." She clapped a hand to her chest. "Oh, my gosh, I just remembered my car is still at the subdivision–at the other house."

"No problem. We'll get it tomorrow," he assured her.

She shook her head, her cinnamon locks swinging wildly. "No, no, you don't understand. We can't go back there. Not tomorrow. We can't show up in town or even near that house for a few weeks, at least. Didn't you hear me tell Daddy we were going on a honeymoon?"

"Honeymoon? But I have to open my shop, Faith. Tomorrow's Saturday. I've got customers waiting for their cars." No customers, no income. Simple math. "I need the money," he said, feeling like a jerk but knowing that now he would have to count pennies even closer than ever.

Admitting his shaky financial condition was humiliating, but Faith had a right to know they weren't likely to be living in high cotton. Not on what he took in repairing cars. Besides, it wasn't like this whole thing had been *his* idea.

His knees ached from kneeling beside her for so long, but he was reluctant to let go of her hands. Just holding them created a warm sensation around his heart. An anchor to reality. The enormity of all that had transpired between them in the last few days was almost more than his poor brain could comprehend.

After the first shock had rocked him, he'd been caught up in the explosive heat of the moment. Like a dream come true, the love of his life would actually become his wife and he would be her rescuer and hero. Happy-ever-after stuff. He hadn't thought beyond the wild excitement of the fantasy until now, when reality slapped him upside the head. Hard.

There was more to it than just being married. More than even the prospect of being a dad. Now he would have to think of someone other than himself—a wife and child. Of their safety, well-being and their reputation in the community. The banker's daughter was actually married to the convict's son. *How about that, folks?* And the ex-fiancé's abrupt personality change was strange enough to make Buddy Lee suspicious and more than a little wary. He wondered if any of them were really safe. Talk about alligators on his ass. Their numbers were increasing.

Faith watched her new husband wrestle with his thoughts and something akin to tenderness welled up inside her. He was such a dear friend. She pulled free from his hands and placed hers on either side of his face.

"I don't want you to worry about the money part, Buddy Lee," she said, looking deep into his dark brown eyes. "My job pays well enough and I've got some savings, plus paid maternity leave. Besides, I never intended for you to support me and my baby without doing my share. It's enough that you've given us your name. That's all I wanted."

When he flinched, she knew she'd said everything all wrong. What she'd asked of him sounded tacky. Selfish.

"I didn't mean...Oh, please, don't look at me like that. I only meant I promise not to be any more trouble. Trust me."

A look of total disbelief flashed across his face, prompting her to lean forward and give his cheek a quick peck. "I've said that before, haven't I?"

After a pause that lasted long enough to make her wonder if he was ever going to answer, he said, "Many times."

The huskiness of his voice and the way his eyes darkened sent a shiver of excitement dancing along her spine. She had the craziest urge to plant a real kiss right on his mouth. What on earth was wrong with her? Probably something hormonal, she supposed, dismissing it as simply part of being pregnant.

"Well," she said, after choosing a slice of nearly-cold pizza and picking the olives off one by one, "here's what we'll do. You go to your shop first thing in the morning, call your customers and have them pick up their cars before ten o'clock, then pack a few clothes and come back here." She popped two of the olives in her mouth. "In the meantime, I'll go shopping for a few things I need and be ready to leave when you get here. Our flight leaves at three-fifteen. We can be on the beach before sundown."

Suspicion flickered in his steady gaze. "And just where would we be going?"

She loved the quirky way his eyebrows twitched when he tried to do the "older brother" act. It was so familiar. Even after all this time, she still felt completely at ease around him. A good thing, since they were a married couple now.

"To Mexico. On a honeymoon." The reservations she'd made at a very private resort would be a perfect hideaway now, as well as compensation for all the trouble she'd put him through. How could he refuse a "thank you" as tempting as a tropical vacation? She'd just cancel Royce's plane ticket and buy one for Buddy Lee. Simple. Besides, who knew what Daddy or Royce might do when she and her new husband returned home?

"The best thing for us to do right now is disappear for a while." She gave him her most persuasive smile. "You do have a passport, don't you?"

Buddy Lee couldn't get his mouth to move. Words stuck in his throat, frozen in place by total shock. His strangled protest finally tumbled out. "Yeah, I got one last year, but Mexico? Have you lost your mind?" His heart kicked into double-time. "For cryin' out loud, Faith! You never said anything about leaving town. There was nothing in the deal about that. I can't go anywhere. Besides, a trip like that will cost a fortune. In case you haven't noticed, my name isn't Rockefeller or Trump. I've got exactly three dollars in my pocket right now, and that's counting all the change."

To prove it, he shoved a hand in his pocket and pulled out two wrinkled bills and a handful of change. "Unless I've won the Lottery and don't know it, I can't even afford to buy your breakfast."

Deep in thought, he walked over to the sliding glass door that led to a balcony and stood looking out into the night, hands clasped behind his back. Mexico. When had she come up with that cockamamie idea? A honeymoon with Faith. On a beach. Under a hot tropical sky. Frosty margaritas and mariachi bands. *Knock it off, Walker, you're fantasizing again.* She's pregnant and this is only a friendly arrangement. The whole honeymoon thing is out of the question. He felt like a husband-for-hire. Well, shoot, isn't that what he really was?

Faith walked up behind him and circled his waist in a hesitant hug. "Don't be mad, Buddy Lee. I guess I wanted to pretend."

She nestled her head on his back. Right between his shoulder blades. A rush of hot desire circled dangerously close to his heart, then shot lower to settle south of his belt buckle as her breathy words scorched right through his shirt. He closed his eyes. *This is never gonna work. Just shoot me now.*

Turning around, he unlocked her arms but kept her hands clasped in his. "Faith, darlin', this isn't one of your 'give-Daddy-a-hard-time' stunts. This is major stuff we're dealing with. Marriage. A baby. The whole enchilada."

"I know, but it seems like such a waste not to use the plane tickets and the resort reservations."

"Doesn't Royce have those?" He was pretty sure the groom usually took care of stuff like that.

"No, the honeymoon was a gift from Daddy, like the house, but I made the reservations in my name. Royce didn't want to be bothered with the details."

When she looked up at him with those soft green eyes full of temptation, he swore the alligators were circling.

"I promise we'll have a good time, Buddy Lee. When was the last time you had an honest-to-goodness fun vacation?"

That was like asking when the last time was he'd had a birthday party. He could answer both questions with one word. Never.

He was totally confused. How could she gush tears like a faucet one minute and be so smiley-faced the next? "Aren't you the least bit afraid your daddy will come tearing after us? Sure wouldn't be hard for him to figure out where we'd gone."

Taking his hand, she led him back to the makeshift bed on the floor and pulled him down beside her. She sat with her legs curled around and leaned in so she could look straight into his eyes. "I never got around to telling him the name of the resort," she admitted. "Or even that I'd picked Mexico as our destination. Royce doesn't know, either, because I wanted to surprise him."

Buddy Lee didn't know whether to laugh or run scared. With her body pressing smack up against him like their being married was as normal as a Texas ninety-degree day, his own temperature soared. If she had any more surprises tonight, there was one in particular he'd like to suggest. Damn straight!

"Mexico, huh?" Well, why not? He'd use the time to figure out what to do about Royce and decide how he was going to support a ready-made family. His life had already spun a three-sixty. Might as well enjoy the ride before he got dizzy and fell off. "What time do we leave?"

"**A**ll I need is for you to keep an eye on the shop for a few days, Scooter. The security alarm's all set. You know the code if you have to get in for any reason."

Buddy Lee held the phone in one hand and flipped through a stack of invoices on his desk with the other while he waited for his friend's answer.

"But, how will I get ahold of you if I need to?" The gravelly voice vibrated in Buddy Lee's ear. "What if somethin' happens, like an emergency?"

He sighed. He'd already explained as much as he was going to, but obviously Scooter didn't think there was enough detail. Oh, he was trustworthy, no question about it, but sometimes his nosiness got to be a real pain in the butt. "Nothing's going to happen, Scooter. I'll check in with you every night, okay?"

"But, where will you ...."

"Scooterrrr ...." He warned, not bothering to hide his irritation.

"Yeah, yeah, okay. I got it, man. If anyone asks, I don't know nothin', right?"

The disappointment in Scooter's voice came through loud and clear, but Buddy Lee wasn't giving in. "Right. And hey, thanks. I owe you one."

Scooter was still muttering when Buddy Lee dropped the phone back in place.

With that business taken care of and the last customer driving out of the service stall, he finally managed to take a deep breath before he checked the time. Hang it all, if they were going to make it to the airport by noon, he'd have to hustle his butt.

Pocketing the day's receipts, he took less than twenty minutes to lock up the shop and get home. Fifteen minutes for a shower, another fifteen to throw some clean clothes in his duffle, and he was on the road to Granite City. But before he picked Faith up at her apartment, he had one more stop to make.

Chapter Five

Yeah, this was Paradise, all right, Buddy Lee thought later that day as he adjusted his sunglasses to lessen the glare of the Mexican sun.

The sleepy little village of *Dos Lunas* lay on the curved beach of a lagoon as aquamarine as any jewel he'd ever seen. Come to think of it, the few jewels he *had* seen were limited to those worn by his customers, most often Beryl Morgan.

With white sands stretching from one end of the spit of land to the other, the solitary atmosphere promised privacy from the intrusion of everyday turmoil. No one hurried. No one wanted to. After only a short time in residence, Buddy Lee discovered that adapting to the slower pace of the village was easier than he'd expected.

Frothy waves licked the edge of the sand, leaving a momentary fringe of bubbles in their wake. Silly sandpipers darted along searching for tidbits while noisy seagulls dipped and chased each other, vying for a choice seafood snack.

From his beach chair, he watched Faith dozing on a nearby chaise lounge, her golden skin bathed by late-afternoon sunlight. His breath hung like dead weight in his chest. The modest one-piece swimsuit she wore clung to her curves tighter than the pink skin of a ripe peach, yet showed no hint of her newly discovered pregnancy. Only the slight fullness of her breasts suggested changes to come, but right now all he could think about was wanting to touch them, kiss them. Damned if his mouth didn't start to water.

Out of necessity he ran down the beach, belly-flopped into the water and swam like he had a great white shark chasing him. No 'gators in saltwater. His arms sliced through the salty waves, taking him away from the temptation that dogged him constantly.

He'd fought with his conscience throughout the entire flight across the border. The inner battle had continued as they bounced along a dusty road in the battered yellow bus, finally reaching the exclusive resort hidden on a crooked finger of land that wasn't even on a map. Reconciling the recklessness of their actions didn't come easy. Justifying their quickie marriage was even more disturbing. But his biggest dilemma was wanting Faith. He swam until the ache went away—temporarily, he was pretty sure. Knowing he couldn't stay in the water forever, he flipped over and back-stroked easily to where the shallow water slid up on the sand, then made his way across the beach to Faith.

He nudged the side of the chaise with his knee. "Better wake up, darlin', before you turn into a crispy critter."

Green eyes opened slowly, squinting up at him. With a smile wide and welcoming, she stretched, cat-like, then patted the lounge for him to sit beside her.

Why does she keep doing that? He wondered if she was totally immune to the jolt of electricity arcing between them. Was he the only one who felt it? Hell, it was strong enough to power a lighthouse.

"Isn't this perfect?" She swept her arms in a wide circle. "It's so private, no one will ever find us."

"Sounds great, but we can't stay here forever." He ran his hands through his wet hair, grabbed a towel and tied it around his waist before he sat next to her. The reason was entirely too obvious.

"I know," she said, "but let's pretend, okay? Just for a few days, let's imagine our world is perfect."

The silent plea hidden in her lighthearted words nudged at a tender spot in his heart. Shoot, hadn't she always wanted to pretend something or other when they were younger? Her pretending had gotten him into some mighty sticky situations, but none as hazardous at this. Back then, it was just a game. Now they were playing for real.

"That would be quite a stretch of the imagination."

They were sitting close enough for his legs, still wet from his swim, to stick to her damp, sun-warmed ones. The fragrance of her coconut-scented suntan lotion mingled with the salty tang of sea spray, blurred his senses with a longing so intense he had to grind his teeth to keep from groaning out loud. At this rate, he was gonna need a bite guard.

She grew quiet and rested her head on his shoulder. There was something disarmingly trusting in the way she relaxed against him, prompting him to slip his arm around her and let his imagination stretch. *So sue me.* His conscience was the only one who heard him.

"At least say you'll try," she implored. "We may never see a paradise like this again."

Isn't that the truth? Thinking about what might be waiting for them when they got back to Liberty gave him heartburn that no antacid could cure. It wasn't gonna be Paradise, for damn sure. But then, neither was this hands-off friends-only marriage.

"You always did like playin' 'Let's Pretend', didn't you?"

He slid off the chaise without waiting for her answer. "C'mon, you've had enough sun. Time to go inside." He grabbed up their belongings, cramming them into the ridiculous fish-shaped beach bag she'd brought along.

When they'd arrived at the resort earlier, she'd insisted on catching the last rays of late afternoon sun, so they'd hurried to the eye-squintingly bright, white sand beach. They had yet to talk about the important stuff. But he planned to correct that oversight as soon as they got back to their room. The one with the king-sized water bed, well-stocked mini-bar and sunken jacuzzi. He rolled his eyes heavenward. *Give me strength.*

Faith hopped up from the lounge and shoved her feet into bright pink plastic flip-flops she'd purchased earlier in the hotel gift shop. Without warning, a tidal wave of nausea flooded her, swamping her with its merciless force. Dizzying brightness flashed behind her closed eyes and she cried out. Buddy Lee grabbed her right before she crumpled in the sand.

The first thing she saw when she came to was the slow-circling blades of the overhead fan. She squeezed her eyes shut and groaned. *Whup, whup, whup.* Even the sound was dizzying.

"Please turn it off. The whole room is spinning."

Perched on the edge of the bed next to her, Buddy Lee jumped up to hit the wall switch and shut the fan off as soon as she spoke. "Holy shi...shoot, Faith, you scared the daylights out of me."

"I'm sorry. I don't know what came over me." She tried opening her eyes again, this time a little slower. The room still spun.

Something bitter and scalding churned in her stomach and rushed up the back of her throat. *Oh, no.* She tried to get out of the bed but her limbs tingled and refused to move.

"Buddy Lee. Bathroom. Quick."

Afterwards, a little weak and totally humiliated, she sipped a glass of ginger ale and took small bites of the plain crackers brought by the concerned housekeeper who appeared after Buddy Lee's frantic call to the concierge.

The Mexican woman had known exactly what Faith needed as soon as she'd seen her in the bathroom, paying homage at the porcelain altar.

"Poor *mamacita*," she'd crooned in broken English as she scurried about. In no time, she had helped Faith into a nightie, settled her quietly in bed with a pat on the cheek and given Buddy Lee a verbal list of instructions complete with arm-waving and head-shaking. He nodded like he'd understood.

Faith watched him thank the woman for her kindness and press some bills into her hand. Hard-earned money from his Saturday customers, no doubt. His easy way of putting others' needs before his own had always been hard for her to understand. Especially when most of the time he had less than the average person. It was common knowledge that before he was sent to prison, Boyd Walker had little concern for his son. Some even suspected there'd been physical abuse, but no one stepped forward to help. Out of necessity, Buddy Lee had learned to fend for himself at an early age.

Her heart stumbled, remembering how he'd always been willing to help her out of her self-inflicted predicaments.

And here he was after all those years, still solving her problems. *He is definitely a better person than I am.*

"Feelin' better, hon?" Buddy Lee closed the door and returned to her bedside.

The sun had already added a healthy tan to his face, but Faith noticed creases of concern wrinkling his brow.

"A little. I'm really sorry I spoiled our first day here. I think I got too much sun." She reached for the cloth the woman had left in a water basin on the nightstand.

Buddy Lee took it from her and used it to gently bathe her forehead. "Being pregnant might have something to do with it, too." His crooked grin delighted her.

"Yeah, that too," she admitted, turning her face to give him better access.

As he lightly stroked the cool cloth along her cheekbones and across her temples, she gave herself over to the soothing sensation. Totally relaxed, she drifted in and out of a dream-like state, allowing air-brushed images that looked suspiciously like Buddy Lee to tease and tempt. Sexy images she wanted to hang on to which suddenly disappeared the minute blunt, slightly rough, and definitely male fingertips traced her lips.

Did she dare open her eyes? What was he doing? It was one thing to be her caregiver for the moment, but this was more care than she'd expected. They were friends, not lovers.

Curiosity won, and she peeked through half-opened eyelids. Nausea was *not* what made her stomach lurch right then. Not what accelerated her heartbeat, either.

Buddy Lee's hand cupped her chin while he stroked her bottom lip with the pad of his thumb. Nothing short of a national emergency could have made her pull away. Frozen in place by the dark intensity of his gaze and the sheer sensual delight of his thumb rubbing her lip, Faith knew there was something going on here that definitely surpassed friendship.

Oh, my! Had he always looked so intriguing? His lean, hard-muscled body did wonderful things to those leg-hugging, bun-defining jeans he'd changed into. Disturbingly dark eyes shot sparks of excitement she'd never noticed before. An aura of subtle temptation radiated around him, captivating her.

She wanted to speak, but her words stopped just short of popping out of her mouth when he leaned over to press a feather-light kiss where his thumb had been.

"I've ordered something from room service. Just some soup." His raspy voice skimmed over the surface of her skin. "You need special attention, Faith. Let me take care of you."

She clung to the side of the bed to keep from dissolving into a puddle of adoration for this man and his tenderness. Darn it. That was all it took to convince her that this was turning out to be a whole lot more than she'd bargained for. Why hadn't she ever noticed his feelings before? Now it was too late to acknowledge them. Her plans for the future didn't include a permanent husband. But how was she going to explain that without hurting him?

"Maybe we'd better wait until later to talk about stuff," he said, moving away from the bed to stand by the window.

"Stuff?"

He rubbed the back of his neck and turned to her. "Look, Faith, we can't keep ignoring the situation. When we get back home, people will have questions. Lots of them, I imagine. I don't have any answers. We need to get our stories straight."

She sat up in bed, and he was relieved to see color back in her cheeks. In fact, she was glowing—as in sunburned. Well, what next? He didn't even want to guess.

"Everyone knows we were friends in school. We'll just let them think we were seeing each other in Granite City," she said.

"Doesn't say much for your relationship with Royce the past year. Makes it look like you were two-timing him." *And makes me look pretty damn sleazy.*

Faith sighed. "I know it's awful, but if we say it happened three months ago, Royce and I weren't engaged then. Most people in town still consider me irresponsible anyway."

"Yeah, and guess what they think of me," he muttered. "Boyd's boy making trouble, just like his old man."

"You didn't make the trouble, Buddy Lee. I did."

She eased her legs over the side of the bed and slowly made her way across the room. The flimsy blue thing she wore just about covered her fanny. Aw, man, what was she trying to do to him? He turned to face the window before he gave in and kissed her again.

Behind him, she slipped her arm around his waist and his whole body stiffened. If she didn't knock that off, there was going to be more than *trouble* made. Right here, right now.

He swiveled, scooped her up and carried her back to the bed. That tantalizing, king-sized, made-for-lovin' waterbed.

"Wha ...." Faith sputtered.

"Don't start, Faith Nicole. I mean it." He sat right down next to her and captured both her hands in his. "We're gonna talk. Now. We've been married since yesterday, and nothing's settled yet. You have to quit pretending. This is real life and, like it or not, we've got a helluva mess going here." He shook his head. "I don't even know why I let you talk me into coming down here. We should be back home, finding you a doctor and dealing with your parents. Instead, here we are in who-knows-where-the-hell Mexico, and you've got morning sickness in the afternoon, not to mention a deluxe sunburn that needs attention."

He brought her fingertips to his lips, kissed them one by one. "Darlin', what am I gonna do with you?"

Unfortunately, what he *wanted* to do with her wasn't even an option, he thought, and went to answer the knock on the door.

"Couldn't we eat on the balcony?" Faith asked after the waiter had brought their dinner tray into the room. "I feel much better now. Honest." The sunset was spectacular, and she didn't want to miss a single minute of it.

The cautious look in Buddy Lee's eyes filled her with remorse. She didn't blame him for not trusting her. All she wanted to do was have these few days to pretend she'd done something right, something normal like everyone else. So far, he was the only normality in her life.

She knew he'd agreed to this unconventional situation only because of the kind of man he was—decent and caring. There wasn't another person in the whole town of Liberty who would've put her welfare above his own. Not one. She squeezed back the hot tears blurring her vision. Some day, she'd make it up to him. Prove to him just how grateful she was.

"Just look out there, Buddy Lee." She pointed to the view from the patio door. "Aren't those colors gorgeous?"

"Yeah, they are, but we've got sunsets back home," he said as he carried their dinner tray out to the glass-topped table on the tiny patio. "Are you sure you're feeling up to sitting out here?"

"Absolutely," she assured him, hurrying to follow. "The fresh air will be good for me." Ignoring the slight tilt of her stomach when she moved too quickly was easier than ignoring the note of resignation in Buddy Lee's voice. She took a deep breath and eased into the nearest chair.

He set a bowl of steaming tortilla soup in front of her and tucked a bright yellow linen napkin across her lap. "No sense messing up that fancy thing you're wearing," he mumbled.

The robe she wore matched her blue sheer nightie but even though it was calf-length, she knew it didn't do much to protect her from his intense scrutiny. She wasn't sure what she'd been thinking when she'd purchased it. Had she still been pretending about having a real-life honeymoon? And had it really only been a few hours since she'd dashed through the mall to buy clothes for her temporary escape to Mexico?

Reflecting on her actions made her wonder if she was mature enough to be a parent. Sometimes she felt like a child who'd never grown up. Did Buddy Lee see her that way? Probably. *He's certainly seen me at my worst, hasn't he?* she thought, remembering how he never even flinched when he'd held her head through that awful episode in the bathroom.. Maybe he was more qualified to be a parent than she was.

"Something wrong?"

He looked up from his soup, careful to place his spoon on the plate and not on the tablecloth.

"This stuff's got quite a South-of-the-Border kick. Is it too spicy for your stomach?" he asked. "I should've remembered where we are and requested something milder, like chicken noodle."

"I'll be fine. And thank you for thinking to order room service. I love sitting out here, looking at the beautiful view." She leaned back in her chair. "Isn't it magical? Like a fairy tale."

He couldn't stop the way his heart softened when she talked like that. When they were younger, there'd been a part of her that longed for a magic carpet ride to paradise. She'd hated the restrictive, small-town lifestyle and her parents' rigid expectations. How he wished he could be her Aladdin with a fancy flying rug to take her away.

He never quite understood her discontent, since a stable family life was all he'd ever wanted. Still, he'd always admired her determination to champion those less fortunate. It was just one of her endearing traits.

"You really like it here, don't you?" He watched her face light up like the neon time-and-temperature sign in front of her daddy's bank.

"I do. It's so beautiful here. I wish we could stay longer."

The wistful yearning in her voice hit him like a fist, and it took all the self-restraint he could muster to keep from whisking her back to that big ol' waterbed in yonder to love her thoroughly and completely until she loved him back. *Walker, you are one messed up man.*

"We have to go back on Monday," he reminded her, though staying here with her was enough to tempt a saint— which he wasn't. "And first thing we're gonna do is make an appointment for you with a doctor. I want to take care of you and the baby, Faith, and I aim to do it right."

She smiled that soft smile again. "We'll have to find someone in Granite City who doesn't know me, or else everyone will find out the baby's real due date. I'll go into the city when we get back, I promise."

Granite City was almost as large as Austin, so finding a competent doctor should be easy. There were plenty of shopping malls, too. "We'll have to buy baby stuff, won't we?" The monumental to-do list spinning in his head was mind-boggling. "I don't know what you need for that, but I'll get whatever you have to have."

Lord, he hoped it didn't cost a fortune. Of course, if push came to shove, he could always sell the Mustang, but that thought purely tore his insides to pieces.

The classic car was his pride and joy, the only thing of value he'd ever owned in his life. He'd poured hours of hard work into restoring it to its original beauty. It was the one accomplishment he'd achieved that was worth anything. The one thing that made him proud. Selling it would certainly put an end to his financial squeeze, but he'd rather lose an arm than lose his Mustang. But if he had to, he'd choose Faith over all of it.

"We won't need any baby things for quite a while. And I can take care of buying those," she said. "Don't worry about it."

"But I do worry. What are we gonna tell people when the baby doesn't arrive when it's supposed to? Everyone will start counting and know we lied. You know how folks are."

"I'll think of something before that happens," Faith said. "I promise."

Why didn't that promise make him feel better?

Chapter Six

Buddy Lee finished his soup and pushed back from the table. "I'd better call Scooter. I promised I'd check in with him. You just sit here and relax. Or would you rather go back to bed?"

"I'll be fine right here."

She waved him off, and he wondered if mentioning the bed bothered her as much as it did him. Not likely. Her hormones probably weren't as riled up as his were. He strode off to find the telephone, swearing darkly as he passed the tempting jacuzzi and damned waterbed. The whole set-up must've been designed especially to test his self-control.

Stabbing in the numbers of Scooter's home phone, he waited impatiently for his friend to answer. After several unsuccessful attempts, he slammed the receiver in frustration. Where the heck was the man? Had something gone wrong at the shop? Scooter never went out on Saturday nights, and the gas station closed at six, so he should've been home.

Worry nipped at Buddy Lee as he strode back to the patio, carefully avoiding the room's tempting furnishings. Damn, he hated being so far away from work. Now he knew why he'd never taken a vacation before. He liked being in control of his own life.

Coming to a halt behind Faith's chair, he stared at the top of her head, her cinnamon curls all tousled and tempting, and stifled the urge to bury his hands deep in those silken tresses. Right then, he knew his life was no longer his own to control.

Faith stirred in her chair but kept her eyes closed. She'd heard Buddy Lee gallumping around in the other room, swearing at the phone and guessed his impatience was caused by Scooter not being available. He was being his usual worry-wart self.

When she heard him stop behind her chair, her pulse skittered. For reasons she had yet to understand, this had begun to happen more often than not whenever he got too close. If she'd wanted to, she would've taken time to examine the situation and determine just what was going on with her nervous system. However, it seemed safer right then to count it as part of her condition. Maybe later she'd work on figuring it out.

When she felt the warmth of his hands on her shoulders, skittering didn't begin to describe the way her pulse danced.

"Did you talk with Scooter?" She knew darn well he hadn't, but couldn't let him know she'd been listening.

He came around and stood where she could see him. "Nope. Guess he was out. I'll try again later."

"Then let's take a walk on the beach," Faith said. "I think a little exercise before bedtime would help me sleep."

"Are you sure you feel like it? You were pretty wobbly there for a while." A frown of concern wrinkled his brow.

"Oh, Buddy Lee, don't be such a mother hen. I feel better now, and it's such a beautiful evening. We might even see those two moons this place is famous for. Let's enjoy it while we can." She rose from her chair headed inside. "Give me a minute to change my clothes."

She wasn't ready to face going to bed just then, wondering if he was thinking about sharing that big bed with her. There wasn't anything wrong with that, she knew. After all, they were legally married, even if it was only an agreement between friends. But how much could she ask of her friend? Had she already asked too much?

Passing the sofa on her way to the bathroom, she realized there was no way that short piece of furniture would hold his long, lean body. She had to admit she'd enjoyed looking at his hard-muscled arms and work-honed torso last night. And today in his swim trunks...well, his other attributes hadn't escaped her notice, either.

Sleeping on the sofa wasn't her idea of comfort. Besides, they hadn't really gotten a restful sleep on the floor of her apartment the previous night, so they both deserved the comfort of that luxurious bed. If she could convince him.

He was sprawled out face down on the bed when she came out of the bathroom wearing a pair of khaki cotton shorts and a yellow tank top. His soft snore broke the stillness, and she debated whether to wake him or not. He looked like a little boy all tuckered out after a hard day at play.

Faith knew that wasn't the case, since she doubted Buddy Lee had ever played much as a child. The few bits of gossip she'd managed to piece together about his early life convinced her that after his mother died, his childhood had been a difficult one. And knowing what she did about his father, she wasn't surprised.

The cushy chair near the bed was the perfect spot to observe him without his knowing. She was tempted to do just that but thought better of it. She really wanted to walk on the beach, and it wasn't all that late.

"Buddy Lee." She shook his shoulder. "I'm ready."

He rolled over, clamped his hand around her wrist, and growled low in his throat. "Me, too."

"What do you mean?" She jumped back, startled by his sudden move and the dazed look in his eyes.

Instantly, he released her hand and sat upright in bed.

"Oh, jeez, Faith, I'm sorry." He raked a shaky hand through his hair. "I must've been dreaming. Did I hurt you?"

The concern in his voice was genuine.

"It's okay," she quickly assured him. I should've let you sleep. We don't have to go for a walk. Those famous two moons are probably an advertising gimmick, anyway."

The waterbed rolled when she sat beside him and all at once, she was sliding, bumping his arm with her shoulder and knocking him back against the pillows. Like a sports replay in slow motion, they rocked back and forth, riding the wavy mattress, and grabbing for each other to keep from toppling backwards on the bed in a tangle of limbs.

Before Faith could right herself, she was wrapped in Buddy Lee's embrace with her face only inches from his. His breathing was harsh and more than a little unsteady. His heart thudded against her own. She saw her reflection in his eyes and thought she read desire in their darkness. Felt her body grow warm beneath his.

Then he slowly dipped his head, and in a move that seemed more right than wrong, she lifted her mouth to his. Whatever else was to come, she knew she wanted this moment to cherish. A moment she might never have again.

Buddy Lee's head swam with the magic of kissing Faith. Better than the kiss they'd exchanged on their wedding day, this one shared more than lips. A lot more. Her soft curves pressed against his hard angles. Her mouth moved seductively under his, tempting—inviting. He swore he wouldn't do more than kiss her, but damn, she tasted so sweet, he wanted this moment to last forever. To hell with going for a walk.

She shifted her hips, and he tugged her closer. It was all he could do to keep from sinking between those silky legs of hers. Instead, he kept his mouth angled over hers, their tongues meeting in a heated, sensuous dance. He tunneled one hand through her hair, cupped the back of her head, and tilted it back just enough to give him access to her throat. He trailed hot kisses to the delicate hollow there, then journeyed down to where the swell of her breasts pushed against the edge of her knit top.

When her fingers dug into his shoulders and he heard a soft whimper escape her lips, he knew he had to stop before something happened they'd both regret. A pain like none he'd ever felt before squeezed his heart with such force he had to move away in order to breathe again.

"I...I'm sorry. That never should've happened," he whispered, pressing both her hands to his chest and gazing into her questioning eyes. "Believe me, I understand the rules of our marriage. Just friends, right?" He doubted his heart would ever beat normally after this. It rocketed around in his chest like a flying saucer off its orbit. Damn, he wanted her.

"F...friends, sure," Faith stammered, pulling her hands free to straighten her clothing and tuck a wayward lock of hair behind her ear. Then with a shaky laugh and a shrug, she said, "We can always blame it on the tropical sunset."

Yeah, right. If the sunsets here were that powerful, Buddy Lee didn't dare watch any more of them. Too dangerous. Faith had every reason to think he was no better than that lowlife Royce Webb. The sympathetic understanding in her voice made him feel like something scraped off the bottom of a shoe.

Dammit, Walker, this is Faith, for cryin' out loud.

She's your friend. What the hell were you thinking? She's pregnant. She asked you for help, not sex.

He stomped out onto the patio in search of a cooling breeze, but got slapped with the hot, humid stillness of the night instead.

He needed to get out of here. Digging in his pocket in search of enough money to buy another beer at the beach bar he'd seen earlier, he froze when his fingers brushed the tiny velvet package he'd put there earlier. Reluctantly, he withdrew the pouch and held it, remembering.

That morning on his way to pick up Faith, he'd dashed into the jeweler's shop in Granite City with his heart in his throat. Not at all sure his meager funds would even purchase a ring worthy of giving her, he had still wanted her to have something more fitting than his heavy class ring.

Spotting a simple gold band engraved with two hearts among the dozens of glittery diamond rings on display, he'd immediately asked the price and discovered happily that it was within his means. He'd intended to give it to her before they boarded the plane, but the opportunity hadn't come up then, so he'd decided to wait... For what, he didn't know.

Now that he'd made a total ass of himself, he didn't think giving her the ring was going to help redeem his standing with her. He was still staring at the little drawstring pouch when Faith appeared at his side.

She pointed to the contents of his hand. "What's that?"

She'd evidently repaired her make-up and combed her hair, because there was no trace of the hot and heavy tussle they'd shared just minutes before. Her eyes held no condemnation, either, but instead, sparkled with curiosity and something else he couldn't quite figure out.

How could she be so calm? Hadn't what they'd almost done in there bothered her at all? Jeez Looeeze! Was he the only one with a libido in overdrive? Or maybe he just didn't affect her in *that* way. Yeah, that was probably it.

Whatever the reason, he was happy to see her smiling. He'd have to live with the fact that understanding her just wasn't gonna happen. Not in this lifetime.

"May I see?" She held out her hand.

Persistent as always, Buddy Lee thought, and nodding, he reluctantly dropped the pouch into her cupped hand.

"Yeah, sure. It's for you anyway." Might as well give it to her. Didn't matter now.

"Really?"

Her eyes lit up like they always did when she was excited. Like they had only minutes before when they'd shared that 'knock-your-socks-off' kiss. Whoa! He couldn't help the hitch of anticipation in his chest or the rush of heat burning his cheeks.

Faith emptied the contents of the pouch in her hand and gave a little cry of delight when she spied the ring.

"Oh, Buddy Lee, it's perfect. Thank you." She threw her arms around his neck in a quick hug, then stepped back as if having second thoughts about getting too close.

"You're welcome," he mumbled. Shoot, were those tears making her eyes all bright and damp?

She fingered his heavy class ring hanging from a gold chain around her neck. "Does this mean you want yours back?"

"Only if you don't want it." She could keep it forever and he'd be happy. "Does this one fit?" He'd made a guess at her ring size and hoped he was close.

When he looked down, she already had it on her finger and the gold chain that held his class ring was tucked safely beneath her shirt.

"Oh, yes, it's just right. Perfectly beautiful." She waved her hand in front of him, then steadied it, obviously waiting for his approval. Her endearing smile touched him, as always.

"Not as beautiful as you, Faith," he said, instantly regretting that he'd spoken his thoughts out loud.

Big, green eyes widened. "That's the nicest thing you've ever said to me, Buddy Lee." She slipped her hand in his. "Can we still take that walk?"

There was something almost sad in the way she looked at him right then. Like she was seeing him differently and wishing he was someone else. He wondered if she regretted her rash decision to dump Royce. No, not Faith. She'd never accept the sort of abuse the man had subjected her to. And Buddy Lee would make sure that never happened again. He didn't give a damn what kind of threats Royce had made. No one was going to hurt Faith. Or an innocent baby. He might not be the perfect choice for a husband and father, but he'd give it his best shot for as long as she needed him. Did he dare to hope for a lifetime?

And he'd keep his hands where they belonged from now on, too, even if it killed him. Their friendship was too important to risk losing it simply because he'd forgotten the boundaries set a long time ago. Being "Boyd's boy" was something he couldn't escape. Not even being married to Faith could change that. He knew he'd never escape the ache in his heart, either, but he would learn to live with it.

Maybe walking was a good thing. If they walked far enough, he'd be too tired when they returned to notice how uncomfortable the sofa was, and hopefully, she'd be too tired to argue with him. "Sure, let's go." He followed her to the door.

A warm tropical night and a walk on the beach with a beautiful girl had the power to stir a man's blood, scattering his thoughts in all the wrong directions. He knew he was dangerously close to telling Faith how he felt about her. He also knew beyond a doubt that he couldn't. Not now. Maybe not ever.

His heavy heart constricted as he watched her walk ahead of him, bare feet kicking up little puffs of sand. Moonbeams danced across the water, bathing her in silvery shadows.

She turned back to him and waved. "Come on, slow poke."

The teasing invitation tempted, but her breathtaking loveliness stopped him right in his tracks as bittersweet longing filled his soul.

If only he could turn the clock back and start this day over. There were so many things he would do differently. More than anything, he wished he could tell her he loved her.

Later, back in their room, the phone connection between Dos Lunas and Liberty crackled and spit in Buddy Lee's ear, but there was no mistaking Scooter's gruff voice on the other end.

"Hey, Walker, 'bout time you checked in. Where in tarnation are you?"

"Never mind," he snapped back. "I just want to know if everything is okay at the shop. I tried to call you last night, but you weren't around."

He was in a foul mood and knew it, but politeness wasn't a priority right then. Not after the miserable night he'd just spent trying to keep from falling off the damned sofa. His aching muscles weren't exactly putting a smile on his face this morning, either. Besides, Scooter didn't need to know any more than the bare details of this pretend honeymoon. Tomorrow afternoon when he and Faith got home would be soon enough to deal with that.

"So, how's it going?" he persisted, since Scooter didn't seem inclined to offer any information on his own.

"Well, other than the security alarm goin' off at your place for no reason, things are okay. The deputy sheriff and one of his boys came and checked everything out. Couldn't find nothin' wrong, so they figured the wind must've tripped the alarm." Scooter wheezed out a cough. "I told 'em the wind wasn't that strong last night, but shoot, nobody ever pays any mind to what I say."

"What?" Buddy Lee snapped to attention at Scooter's matter-of-fact recital of events and fired back a barrage of questions.

"Are you sure nothing was taken? Did you check the Mustang? Hell, I've only been gone since noon yesterday. What do you mean, no wind? How could the alarm go off for no reason?"

"Man, I don't know," Scooter whined. "I went over the whole dang shop. I didn't see nothing that looked out of place. Oh, yeah, I covered the car. Guess you forgot about that in your hurry to get to...wherever."

Buddy Lee's heart skidded into his ribs at the thought of someone messing with his car. The Mustang had a custom-made cover to protect it from scratches or dust. He never forgot to put the cover on after he'd finished working on it. Never. In fact, he clearly remembered checking it twice before he left the shop. An eerie chill fanned the hairs on the back of his neck.

"Where was the cover when you got there, Scooter?"

"On the workbench by the door," came the reply. "Never thought you'd forget something important like that."

Buddy Lee sucked in air between his teeth. "I didn't."

"You mean...?"

"Yeah. Somebody else was in the shop and took that cover off. Are you positive you checked everything?" If someone wanted to mess with his car, how did they get in without breaking a lock or a window?

"Hey, did you check that little window in the back? The one over the...."

"Yep, I looked there first," Scooter said. "I tell you, B.L., if I were you, I'd high-tail it home right away. Things might look innocent enough, but the whole town's buzzin' about the way you two took off right before Faith was supposed to get hitched to Royce. You ain't exactly *numero uno* on the popularity list around here."

"Hell, that's nothing new." He lowered his voice, just in case Faith was listening. The phone was an old-fashioned one, not cordless, so he had to stay close to the built-in desk. He was surprised modern technology hadn't checked in at this fancy, la-de-da resort yet. He turned his back to the patio where she was having breakfast.

"Have you seen Royce around?" He kept his voice as low as he dared. His friend's hearing was less than perfect, though Buddy Lee suspected it was more selective than defective.

Static over the phone lines made Scooter's voice sound like gravel rattling around in a tin can. "Not since th'other night when he gassed up at the station. But Faith's daddy showed up at the shop right after the sheriff got there. He was mad enough to chew nails."

Buddy Lee could just imagine his new father-in-law's rage at finding the shop security broken. That alarm system was one of the requirements for his low mortgage rate. Damn.

"Listen, Scooter, would you stick around the shop the rest of the day? Sort of keep an eye on things 'til I get there?"

"...to work," was all Buddy Lee could make out over the static-garbled connection. Then the buzz of a broken connection hummed in his ear.

He cradled the receiver, sat on the edge of the bed and dropped his head into his hands. If this wasn't the biggest mess he'd ever landed in, he hoped he didn't live to see a bigger one. Convincing Faith they needed to go home today instead of tomorrow was going to take some doing. And some cash to change the plane tickets—if they could even get a flight out on such short notice. Why did everything revolve around money? And why did he never seem to have enough? He could almost understand his father's frustration and reason for the robberies that had landed him in prison.

Whoa, Walker, don't go there. He pulled his thoughts away from that direction. Nothing justified that sort of action, not even living on the edge of poverty. Hadn't he vowed a long time ago never to let himself sink that low in life? He may be Boyd's boy, but he didn't have to turn out like him. No way.

Thankfully, he was his mother's boy, too, and Jewel Walker had given him a code of decency to live by. He wouldn't shame her memory. Ever.

Before he could change his mind, he picked up the phone again and asked the front desk to connect him with the airport. Faith wasn't the only one who could take charge of things. This time, he was making the decision, provided the airline would cooperate, of course.

"**I** can't believe you told them it was a medical emergency," she said as their rickety taxi pulled up in front of the unloading zone of a small local airport. "How did you find out about this airline? I've never heard of it."

Buddy Lee helped her out of the vehicle, then grabbed the bags after the wizened driver unloaded them.

"When the concierge found out our regular airline didn't have another flight out today, he suggested this one. I think his uncle owns it or something. And I told him about your...um, condition," he said, avoiding her eyes.

He counted out the fare to the driver, then followed Faith up a winding gravel path to a quonset hut *Hecho en Mexico* was painted in blinding neon yellow over the entrance.

Faith hesitated at the door "Do you think it's safe?"

Buddy Lee pointed to the sign. "Well, I don't know if that means the building or the airplane was made in Mexico, but this is our only choice if we want to get home today. We'll be fine." He held the door open for her and hoped she didn't hear the anxiety in his voice. He crossed his fingers, just in case.

He had glimpsed a diminutive single-engine aircraft on the runway when they'd bounced up the gravel drive. With bright yellow and purple flowers painted on its side, the plane looked like a huge hibiscus blossom poised for flight. Hoo-boy! He hoped this wouldn't turn out to be a colossal mistake.

Once inside the small plane he held his breath, and Faith's hand, as they taxied down a runway no wider than a sidewalk. Miraculously, the plane was airborne in a matter of minutes.

The pilot, who'd introduced himself earlier as Carlos, leveled off when he reached their cruising altitude and headed toward the Texas border. Relief washed over Buddy Lee with knee-weakening force.

They were half an hour into their trip when Faith asked about Customs. Carlos assured them the flight was legal and there would be no problem crossing into the States.

Oh, terrific. That possibility hadn't even entered Buddy Lee's mind. True to the pilot's word, they proceeded to Granite City, passing through Customs without a hitch.

Faith only became queasy once during the flight, and he was thankful he'd grabbed the left-over crackers from their room and stuck them in his pocket. Between those and the bottled water Carlos provided, Buddy Lee managed to avoid total disaster until he got his wife home safe and sound.

Chapter Seven

They'd been home all of twenty minutes and Buddy Lee was already convinced that only in the loosest sense of the word could his humble living quarters be classified as *home* to someone like Faith Morgan. Faith *Walker*, he quickly amended in his mind. How weird did that sound?

He watched his brand-new wife as she sat at his kitchen table nibbling a piece of cheese and more crackers. Fatigue left dark purple shadows beneath her eyes. Eyes that no longer sparkled, but held the lost look of someone too tired to do more than barely acknowledge the surroundings. She was exhausted, and he knew he should make her lie down and rest. Some husband he was turning out to be. He wasn't doing a very good job taking care of her.

They'd come straight to Liberty after retrieving his truck from the airport parking garage, not even stopping to pick up groceries. He was beginning to think that meals were going to present a helluva problem unless he could find some of those TV dinners in the freezer.

"Listen, um, Faith, why don't you try to take a nap while I check with Scooter about things at the shop? I won't be gone long. I'll stop by the grocery store, too. I think Pac 'n Sac is open on Sundays. When I get back we'll eat and talk about finding a doctor for you. Okay?"

"That sounds wonderful, Buddy Lee. I didn't realize I was so tired." The smile she offered him turned into a yawn and she lifted her shoulders as if to apologize.

When she reached for his hand, the trusting look in those liquid green eyes nearly undid him. His body heat spiked like a hot-wired engine.

For a flash-fire second, all he could think about was falling into bed with her and lavishing her with plenty of TLC—enough to erase all that sadness in her eyes and more than enough to leave them both wildly satisfied. The effort to suppress that urge took the very last fragment of his self-restraint.

He checked to make sure she was resting quietly before he bolted out of the house, hell-bent on locating Scooter. With his life spinning out of control, he desperately needed to find the command switch.

What the heck could've triggered the shop's security alarm? he wondered as he sped toward town. His own suspicions about that tied a knot in his gut. If his Mustang was damaged, by damn, somebody's head was gonna roll.

Faith kept her eyes closed until she heard the door slam and the truck growl out of the driveway. If she hadn't been so wiped out, she would've begged to go along, but for some silly reason, all she wanted to do was sleep. And being in Buddy Lee's bed again created such a deliciously secure feeling, she opted for staying right where she was, in a snug cocoon.

She'd had some other unidentifiable feelings roaming around inside her since they'd returned home, and if her eyelids hadn't been so heavy, she might've tried sorting them out. Maybe later. Right now, the shelter of Buddy Lee's bed was all she needed.

So why did the shelter of his arms suddenly seem so appealing? And why did the memory of that shared kiss cause such heat low in her belly?

Granted, she knew all about the unpredictable mood swings of expectant mothers, but that didn't explain the way her heartbeat elevated when Buddy Lee was around. After all, she was barely pregnant.

The strange part was she'd begun to notice things about him that she'd never been aware of before. His brawny good-looks, for one thing. Okay, so he'd always had a bad-boy kind of appeal as a teen. She'd taken that for granted and ignored the jealous remarks of some of the girls in school. She'd never seen him in any role other than a reliable friend. Someone who liked her in spite of her daddy's money and treated her as if she were ordinary. Their relationship had always been more like brother and sister. Until now.

She punched the pillow and flopped over onto her side. Even with her eyes closed tight, the image of her brand-new husband stayed with her.

She remembered his genuine concern during her first bout of morning sickness at the resort. How he'd slept on the sofa, insisting she needed the comfort of the entire bed. What she'd thought was lack of interest on his part was truly kindness and compassion. Buddy Lee was a good man.

And that was just the beginning of her problem.

Buddy Lee paced the perimeter of the tiny shop office. He'd completed his own examination of the work area and found no clues, but he still wasn't convinced the wind had been the culprit that had set off the damned alarm. How weird was that? Especially after Scooter told him it hadn't been particularly windy last night.

The fact that his friend had found his beloved Mustang uncovered freaked him out. He was absolutely certain he'd left it carefully covered. Absolutely.

"Buddy Lee, I swear nothin' is missing." Scooter waved his hand in the air to include the whole building. "We done checked ever'thing. We went over the whole place. There wasn't no signs of B and E at all."

"I believe you, Scoot, but something tripped the alarm and that makes me suspicious as hell." Buddy Lee pulled out a dog-eared file folder from a battered metal cabinet, flipped it open and thumbed through several yellow invoices. Nothing missing there, either. He jammed it back in the drawer. Hell fire! This didn't make a lick of sense.

Scooter shuffled behind him as he headed for the back of the repair shop where the Mustang was stored.

He examined the car again, inch by shiny inch. Nothing appeared wrong, yet his gut instinct told him someone had messed with it. That cover didn't just fall off by itself. He aimed to get to the bottom of this whole dilemma or die trying. Well, maybe not *die*. He didn't figure that would help matters. Not with Faith waiting for him to take care of her and her baby.

If worry could make a man feel the weight of the world on his shoulders, he definitely was carrying more than his share. He'd bet the farm on that—if he had a farm. All he needed right them was for Faith's daddy to show up, blowing steam out of both ears. He wondered briefly about his own good sense.

The shop door banged shut, and he glanced up at the sound. Well, hell, why not just whack him right here and now?

Lionel Morgan stood there, at least two feet taller than Buddy Lee remembered and looking angrier than a bear with a sore paw. The deputy sheriff was with him, too.

Deputy Elroy Pike was a man of few words and even less patience. "Walker, Mr. Morgan here thought maybe you could shed some light on what happened last night. Something I might have missed. Anything you think I should know?"

By the scowl on his face, Elroy wasn't too thrilled at having to perform a re-run on the investigation. He was also smart enough not to disagree with someone as influential as Lionel Morgan. He just happened to be married to Lionel's niece. Buddy Lee shook his head. "Sorry, Pike, but I'm as puzzled as you are. Nothing's missing, far as I can tell." He wasn't sure why, but it seemed like a good idea not to mention the question about the car cover. At least just then. He'd decided earlier to keep quiet about Faith's rough encounter with Royce. It would be up to her to bring those details to the lawman's attention.

"Appreciate your checking it out, though," he said, making sure to keep a safe distance between him and Faith's irate daddy. The last thing he wanted was another bloody nose.

"If you hadn't abducted my daughter, none of this would've happened." Lionel shook his beefy fist at Buddy Lee. "The deputy has something to say about that, too."

"Hold on, there, Mr. Morgan," Buddy Lee's hands shot out defensive-like, and he backed up a step. No way was he gonna be accused of kidnapping. "There was no abduction and you know that. Faith and I got married legal. By a minister and everything. We told you and Miz Morgan about it right after the ceremony."

The deputy stepped between the two men, facing Buddy Lee. "Did you force Faith to marry you, Walker? Mr. Morgan says she was missing on Thursday night. Know anything about that?"

Buddy Lee's mouth dropped open. "Do I look that stupid?" *Probably not a smart question.* He started over. "Look, Elroy, Faith's an adult. She doesn't even live with her parents, so how could she be missing from there?"

From the corner of his eye, Buddy Lee saw Scooter shuffling forward from the back of the room. Hs silence so far had been an unexpected blessing, but now it looked like that silence was fixin' to be broken. Buddy Lee shot his friend a warning look, but Scooter obviously missed it.

"Aren't you gonna tell 'em about the car cover being moved and all, B.L.?"

Scooter's question grabbed the deputy's attention right quick. The banker's eyes lit up like headlights on high beam.

For a second or two, Buddy Lee harbored a serious thought about permanently silencing his friend.

"What're you talking about, Craddock?" Deputy Pike demanded. "Why didn't this come up in last night's search and investigation?"

Scooter ambled closer, loose-limbed and looking like he knew a secret. "Well," he drawled, "I thought Walker here just forgot to cover the car in his hurry to start on his honeymoon." He rolled his eyes in a 'you-know-how-that-is' look and grinned.

Buddy Lee wanted to punch his lights out. Seriously. There was just so much he was prepared to take from his friend. Hell, he didn't need any more help to hang himself. He just hoped the noose didn't get any tighter before he figured out this mess.

Faith woke up to a room filled with darkness. Disoriented, she sat up in bed, and blinked to adjust her eyes to the shadows. It only took a moment to assess her surroundings. Buddy Lee's bed. A tiny thrill raced through her, accelerating her pulse rate.

She slid from the comfort it offered and smoothed the sheet she'd wrapped around her while she slept. Still warm from her own body heat, the bedding held Buddy Lee's scent as well as her own, even though he hadn't slept there since their wedding. The heady combination caused erotic sensations to blossom beneath the warm surface of her skin, and she placed her hand on her abdomen, reflecting on the tiny life beginning there. A life she was responsible for. She'd asked Buddy Lee to share that responsibility, too, but now she wondered if she'd made the wrong decision.

A sense of apprehension washed over her at the enormity of her action. Could the two of them honestly convince the community of Buddy Lee's part in this scheme? What was going to happen as time passed and her pregnancy didn't show as it should?

And most importantly, was it fair to expect Buddy Lee to keep up the pretense until the baby was born? What if he wanted her to leave before that blessed event occurred? After all, he'd already done his part by giving her and the baby his name. She wouldn't blame him if he had second thoughts about staying.

They hadn't actually discussed the future, either, even though she was aware he'd tried to bring it up. She'd dodged the issue on purpose, something she'd always been good at when she didn't want to face facts.

The frightening thought of facing Royce and his threat of revenge made her cringe. Maybe Buddy Lee thought he could handle those threats, but she didn't like the odds. She'd never intended for him to get hurt. Couldn't bear it if he decided to leave. Suddenly it was important to make certain neither of those events happened, and the reason she wanted him to stay took her by surprise. Could she really be in love? With Buddy Lee? She tucked the unexpected realization away in her mind to examine later.

Halfway to the door, she changed her mind and went to the closet instead. After a quick inventory of Buddy Lee's meager wardrobe, she took a faded plaid cotton shirt from a hanger. In the dresser, she found a pair of knit shorts with a drawstring waist she could pull tight enough to keep from falling off. Garments in hand, she headed for the shower. She wanted to be ready for some serious conversation when Buddy Lee came back. If he came back.

He hadn't meant to be gone so long, but after taking time to inspect his shop, plus all the backin' and forthin' with the sheriff and Faith's daddy, he had given in and let Scooter talk him into sharing a beer back at his friend's double-wide. Now it was after nine, and he was sure Faith was wondering if he'd skipped out on her. Not that he would, but tonight he'd just needed to put some space between them and try to get a grip on this dilemma he'd gotten into.

He hadn't dared tell Scooter the whole crazy story. That would've been like buying a full-page ad in the newspaper. But he needed to bounce some ideas off his friend just the same. Scooter had first-hand access to most of the town's gossip, and if Royce Webb was involved in anything crooked, sooner or later Scooter would know about it.

Buddy Lee desperately hoped Faith was still sleeping but when he opened the back door, he heard water running in the shower. Shit. His chances of avoiding her now were zip.

Too antsy to go to bed, he sprawled on the sofa in front of the television, but instead of turning it on, he stared at the blank screen and let his own fantasies play across the thirteen-inch imaginary stage. Man, oh man, they wouldn't go away. Faith in the shower. Naked and wet. Slick, fresh-smelling skin all rosy and glowing. Soft curves. Tempting. He closed his eyes. Yeah, he could see her now. A floor board squeaked. His eyes flew open. He could see her NOW!

"JeezLooeeze, Faith!" His heart slammed into his ribs.

There she was, standing right in front of him, her delectable curves barely hidden beneath a pair of his old knit shorts and one of his well-worn shirts. The sparkle in her eyes held the familiar glint of mischief he remembered so well. Her hair was still wet, a tangled riot of cinnamon curls just begging for his touch.

"I, um, didn't think you'd mind if I borrowed some clothes," Faith said, padding barefoot across the room. "It was easier than digging through my suitcase." She gave a little shrug.

Next thing he knew, she was sitting beside him, her warm, damp body pressed against his. Her extremely sexy, just-showered scent shot through his bloodstream like high-powered rocket fuel, revving his personal engine at full throttle. No amount of self-control could keep him from reaching for her. And claiming her mouth.

"Faith," he groaned when she placed her hand on his chest.

"I really want to kiss you."

"I know," she whispered, scooted closer, and lifted her face to meet his gaze. "I...I want that, too."

His heart tumbled into her hands.

He was so close to exploding from sheer happiness, he wondered if kissing her would ever be enough.

The kiss started out hot, wet, and open-mouthed, escalating with dangerous speed to something incredibly frightening—and wonderful.

Oh, man, I'm in deep trouble here.

Deeper than he'd ever been, because Faith was kissing him back, slipping her hands under his shirt while her tongue did wild things in his mouth. Before he knew it, he was flat on his back with those sweet curves covering him like a heated blanket.

Did she realize what the hell this was leading to? Fate had to be playing some kind of crazy trick on him, because he could swear Faith was trying to seduce him. And if she kept on touching him like that, he was gonna give as good as he was getting. Oh, yeah. Real soon.

"**B**uddy Lee," Faith murmured against his mouth, "do you want to, um...?" She wished she was better at this sort of thing. Convincing him she was willing to be a true wife wasn't as easy as she'd expected, but she was determined not to make him regret one minute of his decision to help her and her baby. Ever.

She knew being with him would be different than being with Royce, but she hadn't counted on the overwhelming intensity of what she was feeling. Hadn't even known it existed until now. She'd never realized passion could be expressed with gentleness. With Royce, there'd only been roughness.

Yet when she kissed this man who'd been her friend for years, whose concern she'd taken for granted, fireworks went off in places so highly sensitive she was ready to burst into flames. Just a touch—a single kiss from him, and she sizzled from the top of her head to the tips of her toes. When he held her in arms so strong and gentle, she felt totally cherished and protected in a way she'd never known. This was beyond the limits of everyday friendship. More than mere sexual attraction, too. The depth of her feelings for him astounded her. Buddy Lee was *more* than a friend.

She wanted—no, needed—to show him how she felt. He was her hero and deserved whatever she could do to make him happy. And she wished with all her heart that her baby was really his.

"Faith." He groaned her name. "Honeygirl, we have to stop. Now."

His muffled protest hummed in her ear, his hot breath stirred newly discovered cravings of her own. Realizing he was the only one who could satisfy those needs simply added to her unsettled state. She wanted more of whatever was beckoning just beyond her reach. And she wanted it from *him*. Now.

"Why?" she whispered, kissing him hungrily before he could answer. "I'm already pregnant. Don't you want me, Buddy Lee?"

"Aw, sweet Heaven, Faith," he gasped after she gave him another mind-blowing kiss. "I want you so bad I ache, but what about the baby? I don't want to do anything wrong." His breath was ragged, hoarse. "You sure this is what you want, darlin'?"

At the sweetness and devotion in his voice, she nearly wept. Passion and desire rocked through her entire body, and the sudden dampness between her thighs both shocked and excited her.

Her fingers worked to unbutton his jeans, trembled as she slid the zipper down and gazed into his desire-darkened eyes. "It isn't wrong. We're married, remember? And yes, I want this." His jeans hit the floor. His shirt followed, leaving him wearing only his boxers. She stopped his weak objection with another deep kiss.

Without breaking their lip-lock, she wiggled out of her own shirt and heard Buddy Lee's sharp intake of breath when she took   his hands and placed them on her bare breasts. Pleasure did a slow-dance through her nerve endings as he massaged their sensitive peaks with his work-roughened palms.

Bodies naked from their waists up, they strained to touch, to feel, to absorb. His arousal pushed against her thighs, hot, hard and demanding. She straddled him, the thin fabric of their remaining garments proving no barrier for the powerful need rocking them both. Within seconds, his boxers and her shorts joined the growing pile of discarded clothing.

"Oh, God, Faith, you are so beautiful." Buddy Lee could barely speak around the emotion clogging his throat.

He held her tenderly, slowly taking her heavy breasts in his mouth and tugging at their sweetness one at a time until she trembled against him and begged for more. Easing one hand between their bodies, he found her wet and hot, so ready for him he nearly lost it right then and there. But when he would've turned her over and pulled her beneath him, she shook her head.   His breath jammed in his throat. *Oh, please, don't change your mind now, darlin'.*

"Let me," she murmured, slowly lowering herself onto him until the full length of his rigid erection was buried deep within her welcoming softness.

Ah, God! He didn't dare move, just lay there surrounded by her pulsing heat while she kissed him senseless. The torture was exquisite.

Nothing in his lifetime could've prepared him for the way his heart filled with love for this woman. With desire. With hope that his love might be returned. She was his world—and he wanted to be hers.

Gripping her buttocks, he held her motionless until he could no longer resist the temptation to thrust his hips upward. Her cry sounded like a shout of triumph as she matched his moves with a sensuous undulation designed to drive him over the edge.

In desperation, he claimed her mouth and kissed her deeply as their bodies drove into each other with a passion neither tried to subdue. He could barely control the blinding explosion hovering on the edge of his sanity.

Just when he thought he could no longer hold back, she cried out his name and came with such shattering force around him, she brought him to his own paralyzing release.

Buddy Lee slowly opened his eyes in the early morning half-light. Faith slept next to him, her body spooned into his, warm and oh, so soft. One of his arms draped across her waist, the other one was tucked under her and rapidly growing numb. He moved them both, taking care not to wake her, then rolled to the side of the bed so he could observe her more easily while he rubbed the feeling back into his arm. *My God, what have I done?*

His heart ached with the beauty of seeing her in his bed. He'd just experienced the most fantastic hours of his life and his body still thrummed from the intensity of making love with her. In total disbelief that she had been the one to initiate the wild and wonderful intimacy they'd just shared, he let his gaze roam her gloriously naked body. What the hell was that all about? Had he missed a signal somewhere?

She was the best thing that had ever happened to him, but he was afraid he'd just screwed up his chance of becoming a permanent part of her life. Like an insensitive clod, he'd taken advantage of her vulnerable state of emotions. Hadn't he read somewhere that women were often highly sexual during pregnancy? Something about needing to be reassured of their sex-appeal? If he'd been thinking with something other than the lower part of his anatomy, he would have realized the situation was volatile the minute she gifted him with that mind-boggling kiss.

Considering the rough handling she'd gotten from Royce, why had she offered him anything more? Not once had she ever given him the slightest reason to believe she cared, except as a friend. Never encouraged him to hope for any other kind of relationship with her. And he'd been careful not to reveal his feelings, even though he'd almost slipped in Mexico.

He'd really slipped tonight, hadn't he? She would have no doubt now that he wanted her. Man, he was pathetic.

A sudden flash of insight nudged him and he sat up. *Gratitude.* Of course. She'd felt sorry for him and the sex was her way of saying thanks. He should've realized that before his raging testosterone had blown his common sense to kingdom come.

He grabbed his boxers off the floor and stormed into the shower. No way would he let her see how much he was hurting. Falling in love had never been part of their bargain. And he sure as hell didn't want gratitude. No matter how earth-shattering their lovemaking had been, he'd better remember the rules if he wanted to keep Faith and the baby in his life. He wanted that more than ever now. How else could he protect them?

Chapter Eight

The note was propped against a chipped Don't-Mess-With-

Texas mug next to the coffee pot. She saw it as soon as she padded into the kitchen, and had to bite her bottom lip to keep from crying. With her mood already less than jolly, she was teetering on the edge of anger, yet disappointment fed the ache in her heart.

Waking up alone in Buddy Lee's bed was definitely not how she'd imagined this morning would be. Not after the way they had shared the night.

More than a little puzzled by his disappearance, she glanced around the empty room and tried to keep her heart from nose diving. Had she been too aggressive? Too bold? When she remembered his enthusiastic participation, she didn't think so. He'd been totally involved in every aspect of their intimacy.

So what had gone wrong? Why had he slipped out without waking her?

Confused and hurt, she snatched the slip of tablet paper from the counter.

"Faith," he'd written, "Sorry I had to leave early. Coffee is ready. Please rest today. I'll be home tonight. BL"

Terrific. She crumpled the paper, tossed it at the waste basket and missed. Her conscience reminded her that at least he'd had the decency to leave a note, even if he hadn't mentioned anything about last night. What had she expected him to say, after all? Agonizing over it wasn't going to help matters. Or change them.

Tears of humiliation stung her eyes as her highly-charged emotions battled for control of her mood. She'd hoped he would be there so they could talk about what had happened between them. Surely she wasn't the only one who felt they'd gone beyond the boundaries of friendship. Discovered something more.

Deciding to skip the coffee and caffeine until she checked with a doctor, she took orange juice from the fridge instead. She would take care of the matter of finding an obstetrician today while Buddy Lee was at work. She wasn't totally inept.

There was also the problem of her car and clothes to be picked up at the other house, but she could wait until later to do that. Maybe she'd stop by to see her mother, too, even if it meant a chance encounter with her father. The inevitable couldn't be avoided forever. She could handle the situation with her parents, but the fear of running into Royce crawled across her skin like an ugly spider. That was a confrontation she wanted to avoid at all costs.

Phone book in hand, she found the listing for an obstetrician with an office near the interstate and dialed.

Trouble, looking a whole lot like Faith's daddy, barreled out of a black Lincoln Town Car in front of the repair shop just as Buddy Lee finished his first brake job of the morning. There was no mistaking the identity or the mood of the scowling man headed his way. Instinctively, he rubbed his nose.

"Aw hell, here we go again," he muttered and lowered the hydraulic hoist holding the Ford Bronco he'd been working on. He wiped his greasy hands on a coarse shop rag, catching a glance of the sleek automobile as he strode past the front window.

Beryl Morgan was silhouetted behind the dark tinted windows of the town car. A twinge of sympathy for the frail woman tugged at his conscience. How had she managed to live under such dominance for so long? And why? Bittersweet memories of his own mother's plight nudged their way into his thoughts, but he banished them with a shake of his head.

He'd discovered a long time ago that protecting the one you loved was a painful experience. His mother's love for him had caused her one agonizing sacrifice after another. Even at the tender age of six, he'd known a profound loss and sense of guilt when she'd died. And he sure as hell understood the pain of harboring that same kind of protective love for Faith all these years. Being married sure didn't make it any easier. The swamp just kept getting deeper and the alligators bigger.

He braced himself.

"Something on your mind, Mr. Morgan? I'm kinda busy, so unless you want to make an appointment for that Lincoln out there, you'll have to excuse me." He was damned tired of being screwed with.

The burly banker sputtered. "I, ah, you..."

"Yeah?" Buddy Lee prompted, waiting impatiently for the man to say whatever he had to say and leave. His day was going from bad to worse by the minute.

"Her mother isn't well. You knew that when you decided to ruin our lives by taking Faith away. Now, all Beryl does is cry all day long. Her doctor says it's depression." Lionel swiped a snowy white handkerchief across his perspiring forehead with an unsteady hand.

Why, he's an old man. Momentarily shocked by this realization, Buddy Lee quickly covered his surprise. Old or not, Faith's daddy was an unfeeling son-of-a-gun where his daughter was concerned. Always had been.

"That's a damn lie. Faith left because she wanted to." He wasn't going to bring up the subject of the baby unless her daddy did. No sense asking for more trouble.

"Marrying her won't get you a free ride on my money, you know, even if you did get her pregnant," Lionel said, his caustic words edged with arrogance.

"Never thought it would," Buddy Lee snapped back. *Of all the damn fool ideas!* He almost argued the point about the pregnancy, but for once his good sense kicked in on time. He turned and walked away instead. Didn't need to hear any of this crapola again.

"Wait!" Lionel hurried after him. "How much would you take to have the marriage annulled? To give up your right to the child? I'll write you a check right now."

Buddy Lee spun around so fast he left his good sense behind. Otherwise he wouldn't have put his tender nose in the line of fire again. But he planted himself right in front of his adversary, leaned forward and stared him straight in the eye. Even though his hands itched to shove the man's degrading words down his throat, for Faith's sake he restrained himself.

"There isn't enough money in the whole world to turn me into that kind of low-life. Walker's my name, but, by God, it's Buddy Lee, not Boyd. I'll take care of what's mine and that includes Faith and the baby." Anger boiled in his blood, spewing out on his hard-bitten words. "Morgan money has never interested me, so you can take your bribery and stuff it...sir!"

Lionel shook a beefy fist at Buddy Lee's face. "Be careful," he warned, "or you'll wind up a no-account loser, just like your old man."

With a final curse, the furious banker stomped out of the shop, leaving Buddy Lee feeling like he'd just tangled with the granddaddy of all alligators. Damn!

The long walk from the house to the subdivision where she'd left her car on Thursday gave Faith a chance to reflect on the extraordinary results of her impetuous wedding and subsequent honeymoon in Mexico. Results she'd never expected in a million years.

When she'd asked Buddy Lee for help out of sheer desperation, she'd anticipated a little resistance from him, but remembering how he'd stuck up for her in the past, she'd been pretty sure he'd help her out of this sticky situation, too. After all, it wasn't like she was asking him to be her mate-for-life. She didn't even want a long-term relationship, since her choices of partners kept turning out to be jerks. Besides, having this baby was going to be enough of a challenge.

So what was this 'thing' happening between her and Buddy Lee? Hot sex was no reason to start imagining anything beyond friendship. Okay, maybe her gratitude *had* gotten a teensy bit out of control, but his reaction had bordered on shocking. Over the top. Her thoughts sped down that path of remembered pleasures—and the side trips he'd taken her on. Trips she'd never experienced before until now. Who would've thought she and good ol' Buddy Lee could get it on like that? Or that they could generate sparks hot enough to ignite a flame like gasoline spilled on a brush fire.

Either the walk had exerted her or her imagination was working overtime, because by the time she reached the house, her heart was racing just thinking about the possibilities that might occur in the night ahead.

One look at the empty driveway, though, and her thoughts segued into a whole different zone. Where was her car? Why wasn't it parked in the driveway where she'd left it?

She raced up the steps, yanked on the door. Of course, it was locked. She remembered leaving her key on the hall table when she'd fled. Dumb, dumb, dumb, she chided herself.

And since Daddy's idea of high-security measures had been to omit any windows in the garage, she couldn't tell if the vehicle had been put away or not. She chewed her lip in frustration.

Angry with herself for leaving the car in the first place, Faith sat down on the steps and tried to come up with a plan. She'd always been good at planning. *Think.* There had to be a solution. All she had to do was rationalize and think. She was deep in concentration when a familiar male voice sent her stomach plummeting.

"Lose something?"

Ohmygod! She jumped up, ready to run, as Royce appeared from the back of the house.

His silent-footed approach felt predatory, and the cold contempt she glimpsed in his eyes as he drew closer pumped adrenalin through her veins at break-neck speed.

"What did you do with my car?" Her voice faltered only a little. Desperation fueled her grit. Kept her focused.

"You shouldn't have run away, Faith," Royce said in a voice too smooth to be sincere. "I looked everywhere for you." He reached out and circled her wrist with his fingers. Tightened them like a steel trap.

She knew it was useless to try to pull away. Instead, she elbowed her arm into his chest, twisted hard and jerked free from his grasp before he had a chance to react.

Panic pushed her to ignore the stitch in her side and keep running. Royce's angry shouts followed her as she dashed down the street, not daring to slow down. She placed a protective hand on her stomach and prayed no harm would come to the baby.

The entrance to the subdivision was almost in front of her when her foot caught on a stone. Stumbling, she flung her hands out to keep from pitching forward just as Royce caught up with her and snaked his arm around her from behind.

"Why do you keep running?" he whispered, his mouth much too close to her ear.

"Please, I..."

He squeezed her middle so tight she could barely breathe. Black spots danced before her eyes.

"Answer me." Harsh words seared her skin. "Explain how you two-timed me with that white trash. How you let a convict's son get you pregnant." With a swift jerk, he pulled her against him. "You little bitch," he rasped. "Make a fool out of me, will you?"

Twisting her arm behind her, he pushed her back along the sidewalk.

Swallowing hard, Faith struggled to keep from passing out. She had to stay focused. Had to get away. Dear God, Royce's anger was the very thing she's been afraid of. His temper flare-ups had become more frequent during their relationship, but never as volatile or as threatening as this.

"Royce, please don't do this," she pleaded. Frantic, she surveyed the development's empty streets, heart sinking and hope fading. There were no occupants in the newly-built houses yet. No one nearby to hear her cry for help.

Royce shoved her into the house, and she screamed anyway. And when the back of his hand struck sharply across her mouth, she cried out again, tasting the blood from her split lip. His crushing hold on her wrist was the only thing keeping her from falling to her knees. Tears of pain gathered in her eyes. Blurred her vision.

"You're hurting me."

"Shut up! That bumbling grease-monkey you married can't help you now." His eyes narrowed to sinister slits.

The threat she saw in them sent chills of terror coursing through her. Dear God, he was right. Buddy Lee had no idea where she was. How could he or anyone else help her now? Why hadn't she told him all of the truth instead of only part of it? Now it was too late.

Dammit, I told her to stay put. After searching every room, Buddy Lee stormed from the house. He'd come home to find Faith gone, and now he scanned the street in frustration. Was it so hard for her to do as he'd asked? He'd only been thinking of her health. Her safety. She needed to take it easy and avoid stress. That's why he'd brought home take-out chicken for their lunch. The reason he'd closed the shop for an hour at noon to check on her, something he'd never done before. But then, when had she ever stopped to consider the consequences of her impulsiveness?He paced the porch, hands stuffed in his pockets. When the thought hit him, he slapped his forehead and ran for his truck. *Her car.*

She could be stubborn as a sticker-burr when it came to getting her own way. Probably walked clear over to the subdivision in this blasted heat, too. Grinding gears, he down-shifted and headed in the direction of the subdivision.

Faith hadn't changed much in the years he'd known her, he reflected as he took the first corner on two wheels. Act first, reason later, had always been her M.O. when they were younger. By the looks of things, she was still impulsive. And that was exactly why she needed him now, even if she didn't know it yet. Why he couldn't get rid of the fist of fear balled in his gut.

He would've driven right past the empty-looking house if he hadn't seen the shadows of two people in the curtainless bay window facing the street. He slammed on the brakes, cut the engine and raced to the front door.

"Faith, you in there?" He pounded his fist against the paneled oak. "Faith?" He could hear raised voices – someone's cry. Dammit all, what was going on? "Faaaith!"

Still shouting, Buddy Lee sprinted around the house, rammed the back door open with his shoulder and barreled straight into the corporate-suited figure of Royce Webb.

Royce had Faith pinned against him, one arm around her waist, the other hooked under her chin.

Buddy Lee saw red. "What the...?"

Fear glazed Faith's eyes. "Run, Buddy Lee. Get out before he hurts you, too."

Fury propelled him forward. He flew at them, swinging and cussing. "Webb, you lousy... Uummph!"

Royce chanced a jab with one hand, but Buddy Lee deflected the blow with his shoulder.

"Let her go. Now!" He wrenched Faith loose from Royce's grip, then pushed her out of the way right before he sent the other man to his knees with a jab to the gut.

Royce doubled over. Buddy Lee yanked him up by the shirt front and hammered another blow to his jaw. The crunch was loud enough to assure Buddy Lee his aim was right on target.

Royce grunted, staggered to his feet and swung wildly. A lucky punch thwacked across Buddy Lee's face. Blood spurted and he grabbed his injured nose, losing his focus just long enough to give Royce a chance to ram his lowered head into his ribs.

"Stop it, stop it!" Faith jumped between them, clawing at Royce and screaming.

"No, Faith, get back!" Buddy Lee tried to push her out of harm's way, but she ignored his warning shout.

Royce bellowed when her nails raked down his cheek. "Get the hell off me!"

One ruthless slash of his open hand sent Faith reeling across the room. She crumpled to the floor with a moan.

Enraged, Buddy Lee plowed into Royce like a madman.

"Bastard!" His last swing went wild and his fist glanced off the side of Royce's jaw. Royce staggered and bolted for the door.

Buddy Lee scrambled over to where Faith leaned against the wall. When he gathered her in his arms, she melted against him with a sob.

"I...don't feel so good," she murmured into his torn, bloody shirt.

"C'mon, darlin', I'm taking you to Doc Sutter." He scooped her up in his arms, wobbling a little on his not-so-steady legs.

"Nooo, not him." Faith's small fist thunked Buddy Lee's chest. "I made an appointment next week with a new doctor in Granite City. Everyone in Liberty goes to Doc Sutter."

Buddy Lee ignored her weak protest. "Granite City's too far away. You need attention now." He helped her into the truck, making sure her safety belt was buckled before climbing in and shoving the key in the ignition.

Tamping down the sense of urgency that made him want to imitate a NASCAR driver, he white-knuckled the steering wheel and concentrated on keeping the truck under the speed limit.

Unfortunately, his brain waves kept rotating back to Faith and how close she'd come to getting seriously hurt.

"What the hell were you thinking?" he blurted.

The instant the words were out, he regretted them, but he was so damned angry the hot burst of fury rushed ahead of his good sense. Next thing he knew, he was shooting his mouth off without thinking.

A sideways glance at Faith sitting rigid and silent next to him told him he'd hurt her feelings. But what if Royce had managed to take her away before he'd gotten there? What if she'd been badly injured...or worse? What if he hadn't gone to the house in the first place? The *what-ifs* still crowding his brain pure-D terrified him. *What if he'd lost her?*

He hadn't meant to lose his temper. Not at her. But seeing Royce manhandle her had been more painful than having a knife plunged into his heart. He was still reeling from the impact of that scene. That was no excuse for the way he'd just hollered at her, though. No excuse for acting like a jackass, either. *Boyd's boy* was living up to his name. Doing a sorry job of being a friend, too.

Aware that his harsh words were the cause of the tears leaking from the corners of her eyes, he had to try to make amends somehow. Had to show her he wasn't like Royce in any way, shape or form. But how?

"Faith?"

She didn't answer him. Just hugged her arms tight across her chest like she trying to keep her feelings from escaping. What was she thinking? That he was as awful as Royce? Guilt weighed heavy on his conscience.

"Faith, hon, I'm sorry for yelling, but when I couldn't find you at home, I panicked. And when I saw Royce hurting you ...." His words trailed off into the silence surrounding them.

"I know," she whispered. "I know."

The sadness behind her words cut through to the very core of his soul. A simple apology wasn't going to be enough. How much damage had he done to their fragile relationship?

Without another word she slipped her hand under his and some of the heaviness in his heart lifted. She kept it there until he stopped the truck in front of the doctor's office and he reluctantly drew his away to turn off the ignition.

She looked at him then, green eyes as promising as the first buds of spring, and the sweet forgiveness in her smile made his heart swell with hope. Gently, he brushed his lips across her bruised ones and knew he could never love her more.

With his arm firmly around her, they made their way up the walk.

Chapter Nine

"**Y**ou're lucky you caught me before I went upstairs for lunch," the doctor said as he opened the front door and ushered the pair into the waiting room. "Had some stitching up to do on Mary Brady's youngest. Caught his leg on a barbed wire fence chasing after his dog." He clucked his tongue. "Kids."

Noel Sutter's smile was warm, reflecting the deep affection he had for his patients. One of the reasons he was so popular with them.

He motioned toward the half-circle of chairs opposite the unoccupied desk where his nurse usually sat. "Now, you go ahead and get comfortable, Buddy Lee, while I take Faith with me and see what this is all about. There's magazines to read in the rack. Nothing about cars, though." He spread his hands in apology.

"That's okay, Doc, I'm too wired to read."

The doctor eyed him intently. "I'll take a look at that nose of yours, soon as I finish with Faith." He led her into the next room.

The doctor's office occupied the lower floor of a restored, two-story Victorian house two blocks west of town. At one time, it had been the home of the town founder, but when the last of the heirs died, young Noel Sutter had purchased it and opened his medical practice. With his living quarters on the upper level, he was on call twenty-four hours every day. Had been for forty some-odd years. It was a known fact that everyone in town rated him right up there next to the Almighty.

Faith accepted Doc Sutter's help as she walked into the examining room. She couldn't remember a time when he hadn't been there for her. He'd treated every childhood ailment she'd ever had and bandaged innumerable scrapes and cuts. Answered her questions when her mother had been too embarrassed to discuss the facts of life with her. He knew her as well as her own mother did. Better, in fact. And that was the very reason she hadn't wanted to come here. Some of the things he knew were extremely private.

"All right, young lady, let's have a look at you," he said.

He took her blood pressure and checked her pulse. Put his stethoscope to her chest and listened. Gently examined her bruises and swollen lip, then wrote on her chart.

His calm, methodical movements immediately eased her misgivings and she relaxed. The doctor was her friend. She could trust him.

"Now, my dear," he said, his kind smile reaching his eyes, "why don't you tell me what this is all about?" He laid his instruments aside and pulled up a stool. "I hear you and Buddy Lee got married. Guess the whole town knows it by now, eh?"

She nodded. Why couldn't she bring herself to say anything? Noel Sutter would never be judgmental, but she was humiliated to have him see her like this. Again.

"Your injuries are minor, Faith, just a few simple abrasions. Nothing that needs stitching. But the bruises look a mite familiar." He raised his eyebrows, his gaze lingering on her face. "Did Buddy Lee...?"

"Oh, no. No, of course not," she interrupted. The last thing she wanted was for Buddy Lee to take the blame for any of this. "I...fell."

Noel Sutter raked a hand through his shock of white hair. "I may be old, child, but I'm no fool. The last time I saw you with bruises on your arms and neck like these, you admitted it was Royce Webb who'd put them there. Didn't I warn you then to be careful? To seriously consider ending that relationship?"

Faith felt the start of tears—the burning ache in her throat. She pressed her sore lips together to stifle a sob.

The grandfatherly doctor placed a comforting hand on her arm. "I'm here if you want to talk about it."

His gentle words broke the dam holding back her tears. She gave in and let them flow. All the tension of the past few weeks burst through her tightly controlled emotions as she related the events that had sent her to find Buddy Lee and ask for his help.

When the storm of confession finally passed, she took the tissue Doc offered, mumbled her thanks and wiped her eyes.

"You know I'll need to examine you, Faith," he told her. "To make sure the baby's all right. You were knocked around pretty hard. My nurse, Molly, won't be back for another twenty minutes. Why don't you rest here until then?"

"I don't want anyone in town to know the truth."

"I understand. What you've told me here will never leave my office. And I assure you, Molly Higgins is trustworthy. The baby's welfare, and yours, are my priority now. But if it happens again, I'll insist you go to the authorities." He took her hands in his, patted them. "I've known you since you were a youngster, Faith. Despite the fact that you were headstrong and impulsive, you've always had a loving heart. This baby needs you as much as you need it. And for what it's worth, I think Buddy Lee is a fine choice for a husband and father. Promise me you'll be careful and stay away from Royce. You did the right thing when you left him."

Faith nodded and took the paper gown he handed her.

"I'd better give your husband a little man-to-man support now. Be back with Molly in a few minutes." With that, he left the room.

Faith put the gown on and waited, deep in thought. Doc Sutter spoke the truth. She did need this baby to love, but how was she going to straighten out the tangle of deceit she'd managed to trap them both in? And how was she going to keep Royce from finding out the baby was his? She wouldn't blame Buddy Lee if he backed out of their agreement...and marriage.

Royce Webb thought he was going to die right there in the alley next to the bar. Nausea swirled in his belly, but he was too scared to move. The gun pressed into his side belonged to one of Boots Ogden's goons, and Royce's gut heaved when the man rammed the automatic into his ribs for the second time.

"A few more days, that's all I need!" His words slurred around the metallic taste of fear coating his tongue.

"The boss don't like late payments, dude."

Stub Peabody had the build of a bull moose, thickset and dense. Royce knew the thug's mentality was equally dense, but when someone the size of a mountain shoves a gun in your gut, it's smart not to argue. The fierce desire to remain alive severely limited his ability to think rationally.

"I'll get the money, Stub. I promise. Just ask Ogden to give me another week. Only one, that's all I'm asking."

Sweat slid down his forehead into his eyes, stung like hell. He wanted to wipe them, but didn't dare lift his hand. God, he wanted a drink. Needed one to keep from losing his nerve. His mouth was so dry he couldn't work up a good swallow, and he had the shakes bad.

Stub poked the weapon under Royce's chin. "Why should I, pretty boy? What's in it for me?"

Royce tried to swallow and felt the cold tip of the gun barrel nudge his Adam's apple. *Think, dammit! Think of something fast.*

What would a hood like Stub want that Royce could get his hands on fast? Women were a dime a dozen at Ogden's palatial estate near Lake Charles, Louisiana. The casinos drew them like bees around clover, and Ogden's boys had their pick of them. Between women and expensive booze, there wasn't much else that would interest this bull holding a gun.

"I'm waiting," Stub growled. "I don't like waiting."

In desperation, Royce blurted out the first thing that came into his panicked mind. "A car. I can get you a car. How about a classic Mustang? You know, the real thing? You'll have chicks falling all over you. What do you say?"

Shit, what had he done? His mind reeled. He'd just promised Walker's Mustang to the idiot, when he'd planned on having it himself. But he was in no position to argue right now. He had to save his own skin.

The goon pursed his thick lips, shaggy eyebrows snaking into a dark scowl. "A Mustang, huh? How do I know you're not just jerking me around?" He chucked the .38 a little harder into Royce's throat.

"I...I wouldn't lie to you." Royce fought the urge to gag. His voice shook so bad he could hear the tremors in every word. They coursed through his entire body, churned in his stomach, rattled his concentration. What if he couldn't convince this oversized knucklehead? He licked his dry lips. He didn't want to die.

"It's a beauty, honest," he whined. "A '65 Mustang in mint condition. Worth a damn fortune. We can make a deal, if you'll buy me a little time with your boss." His heart pounded like a jackhammer in his chest. If this ruse didn't work...He held his breath and tried not to think about the consequences.

Stub studied him through cold, gray eyes for a long time before he nodded slowly and tucked the .38 inside his jacket. "Okay, pipsqueak, but two days is all you get. Deliver the car to me, plus the money you owe the boss, by day after tomorrow, or else."

Royce stiffened his legs to keep from collapsing. Two days. Sweat streamed from every pore in his body, while fear crawled around in his gut like a worm. He had to agree—or die.

"Okay, okay," he stammered. "It's a deal. Where do you want me to meet you?" He could barely push the words out between his chattering teeth.

Stub shot him a deadly glance right before he lumbered down the alleyway toward the street. "Don't worry, Webb," he said in a tone so menacing, Royce almost wet himself. "I'll find you."

The promise sounded like a death knell. Royce watched Stub leave, afraid to breathe, afraid to move until the dark sedan slid away from the curb. Then he dropped to his knees and cried like a baby before he headed for the bar.

"Hey, sugar, what brings you to this side of town?"

The inside of the tavern was dark and smoky, the sparse noon crowd beginning to thin, but Royce didn't need bright lights to recognize the throaty greeting of the hip-swinging blonde advancing across the room like a heat-seeking missile.

"Hello, Didi." He concentrated on his drink and purposely avoided her question. Lifting the glass to his lips, he closed his eyes and let the first gulp of whiskey burn its way slowly down his throat. Without opening his eyes, he tossed back another and waited while the heat spread through his system.

When his nerves finally began to smooth out, he allowed himself a brief survey of the room and breathed a sigh of relief when he saw he hadn't been followed. He aimed a nod and a two-fingered motion at the bartender. Another double appeared in front of him before he had time to blink.

Gripping the glass to steady his still-shaking hands, he was thankful he'd been only a few steps away from the tavern door—and a drink. The liquid courage in his glass finally started to kick in, so he shifted his attention to the woman.

Didi hitched herself up on the bar stool beside him and ran one long, dark-red fingernail down his arm. "You look a little strung out, Webb. I know a much better way to calm your nerves than drinking, hon." She lowered her thickly-mascara'd lashes and gave him a suggestive smile. "It's been a long time. I've missed you."

"Yeah. I've been busy." He sipped his drink, slowly coming down from the high of total panic that had sent him rushing into the tavern after he'd finally stopped blubbering. He'd been too close to ending up with a bullet in his head. That frightening image kept spinning around in his brain, along with the urgent need to come up with a scheme for getting his hands on Walker's Mustang. He needed money fast. Ogden wasn't going to wait much longer. Casino owners rarely did.

The blonde walked her fingers up Royce's arm and stroked his cheek. "Too busy to stop by once in a while?"

She leaned closer, swiveling the bar stool so that her breath swirled hot against his ear and her breasts brushed his forearm. "I thought for sure you'd be knocking on my door. Especially after the way Faith dumped you for Buddy Lee." She made a little sympathetic sound. "You know, if my fiancée was pregnant with my kid and ran off to marry somebody else, I'd be downright pissed." The tip of her tongue began a moist journey around her pouty lips. "She made you look like a chump, Royce. Or didn't you want your kid? Was that the problem?"

He jerked around, not sure he'd heard her correctly. "Say that again. *My* kid? That's impossible. She was playing around with that white trash, Walker, before we were ever engaged." His fingers dug into Didi's shoulder. "Where did you hear that wild idea?"

Didi shrugged out of his grasp. "Hey, not so rough. I don't owe you anything, anymore. You dumped me, remember?" She sipped her vodka and tonic, eyeing him over the rim of her glass like a cat watching a mouse.

His head pounded ruthlessly, and his nerves started twitching all over again. What the hell was going on? The baby was *his*? If this was true, why was Buddy Lee involved? It made no sense.

"Don't play games with me, Didi." He lowered his voice to a menacing whisper. "What kind of proof do you have that the baby is mine? Where'd you get your information?"

"Like I said, I don't owe you." She angled her head provocatively and looked at him through lowered lashes. "But I might be persuaded to share more than information, if you know what I mean." She wet her lips again, the pink tip of her tongue exposed just enough to convey a graphic invitation. "My place?"

Royce regarded her carefully. He couldn't afford to take the chance of missing something as important as this, but his former lover had been known to twist the truth a time or two. Still, he remembered she'd been damned good in the sack.

"If you're lying, you'll regret it." He downed the last of his drink as the germ of a plan took shape in his mind, a scheme that could have Walker handing over his car without an argument, if he played his cards right.

He'd made easy work of checking out the shop when Walker and Faith had been out of town. Simple procedure for someone with his expertise at covert B & E's. He'd nearly gotten away with taking the car right then, but he'd miscalculated his time frame, and the damned alarm system kicked in before he had a chance to disarm it. But now he wasn't going to have to break in after all. He mentally cheered. By the time he put this clever plan into action, Walker would be begging him to take the car.

Royce chuckled under his breath. Sometimes his own brilliance astounded him. By selling the car to pay off his loan to Ogden, he'd save his own neck and have money left over to leave the state. There was only one little hitch. He'd have to steer clear of Stub and make sure to get out of town before the goon realized he'd been double-crossed. That might take a little thought, but it wasn't impossible.

The rest was a piece of cake. He really didn't care whether Faith's rug-rat was his or not. The kid was just a bargaining point. Besides, he'd be long gone before anyone noticed him missing. He'd drop the car off in Lake Charles and take a plane to the Bahamas. Perfect.

Didi shot him a sly look. "I don't need to lie. My kid sister has a part-time job in Doc Sutton's office filing medical records for him." She rested one hand on Royce's thigh, let it slide toward his crotch and linger briefly. "I can get you all the proof you need, sugah. And my price is negotiable."

With a heavy-lidded wink, she eased off the bar stool, straightened her minuscule skirt with a yank and, hips swaying like a backyard swing, sashayed out of the tavern on a cloud of heavy magnolia fragrance.

Royce tossed some bills onto the bar and followed. With his nerves tranquilized by whiskey and his sexual appetite whetted by Didi's voluptuous curves, he was more than ready to negotiate.

Buddy Lee helped Faith out of the truck when they reached their house, determined to wait until she'd had time to rest before questioning her about her conversation with Doc Sutter.

He hadn't intentionally eavesdropped. Hell, the door to the examining room had swung open a crack. Old doc's voice was about as quiet as a fog horn. Faith's own words hadn't exactly been hushed, either, and his attention had zeroed in on what he knew was a private discussion the minute Doc mentioned Faith's previous bruises and their cause.

The temptation to charge into the examination room and demand the entire story had nearly catapulted him out of his chair. Thank God for the tiny bit of common sense that had kept him in place. And for Doc's calming, but sparse, words of explanation. As soon as Faith felt better, he was damn well gonna ask for more details.

"You need to lie down." He supported her with one arm and opened the screen door with the other hand.

Pale and shaky, she leaned on him as they walked, but he barely felt her slight weight against his own injured rib. The worry about her health as well as her safety consumed him.

"Maybe I'll just rest on the sofa for a while," she said.

"Huh-uh. Too many hard lumps. You'll be more comfortable in bed."

A faint smile teased the corners of her mouth. "Weren't you the one who insisted the sofa was fine for sleeping?"

He grimaced. "That's different. I'm not expecting a baby. Physically, I mean."

She laughed quietly. "Well, that's a news flash."

The warmth of her laughter gave Buddy Lee a brief glimpse of what their life together might be if their marriage had been the culmination of shared love instead of the result of an old friendship.

He watched, hypnotized, when she stopped to fuss with a tiny arrangement of yellow and white daisies on the lamp table next to the sofa. He couldn't ever remember having flowers anywhere in the house. Now, they blossomed in every room, thanks to Faith. In the few days since their wedding, she'd managed to turn the tiny house into a cozy nest, a safe haven away from the reproachful eyes of the community.

That same censure had dogged him for years. *Boyd's boy* had lived under the town's scrutiny his entire life, and he still struggled to escape the stigma of his father's name.

Amazingly, Faith seemed completely at ease amidst the sparse furnishings in the little tract-house. Better than he managed to fare on his infrequent visits to the Morgan mansion. Their worlds were poles apart, yet she had adapted to his without a hitch. He would never fit into hers. Didn't even try.

The room suddenly shrank, and the image of Royce holding Faith captive flashed across Buddy Lee's mind. Whatever the price of her safety might be, he vowed somehow to provide it. Now, more than ever, she was his responsibility. The fact that he loved her totally and completely only made him more determined than ever to prove his worthiness. But it was beginning to look like *Boyd's boy* was never going to rise above his daddy's reputation.

"You really should take it easy, Faith. Remember what Doc Sutter said." He placed a guiding hand on the small of her back and gently coaxed her into the bedroom.

"Think of the baby," he quickly added, feeling guilty because he'd been more concerned about her than the child she carried.

"I think about it all the time," she admitted with a sigh.

Her remark jogged his heartbeat up a notch, and he switched the conversation to a safer topic. "I'll bring you something. Maybe the chicken I brought home earlier is still edible."

One eyebrow quirked at him. "What about your sore ribs? You should be the one to rest." Hesitantly, she touched his side.

Her fingers were heated probes shooting electric currents through his body. Jeez Looeeze. He forgot he even *had* ribs for a moment as other parts of his anatomy claimed his attention.

"Aw, I've had worse," he said, playing down his injuries and trying to keep his voice calm. If he laid down beside her now, there'd be no rest for either one of them. Knowing that, he stepped back to keep from putting his own needy hands where they didn't belong. His promise to take care of Faith sure as hell didn't include sex.

Even though he stood a good two feet away from the bed, he could still feel the sizzle of her touch. What was wrong with him? She'd been hurt, for cryin' out loud. Abused and threatened by a sorry piece of humanity with no conscience and the morals of a tomcat.

And that reminded him of the question he wanted cleared up, as soon as he brought Faith something to eat.

"Be right back." He retreated to the kitchen, leaving her lying in bed, a puzzled look on her drawn face.

He hurried to rustle up a handful of potato chips to add to the cold fried chicken he'd arranged on a paper plate. Not very appetizing, he thought, grabbing an apple from the fridge and adding it to the quickie meal. After pouring a glass of milk, he carried the meager offering into the bedroom.

Faith looked at the single plate, then at Buddy Lee. "Aren't you going to eat, too?" She wasn't certain if she could keep the food down. Her stomach felt like one of those wave-machines at the water park.

"I'll grab a chicken leg before I go back to work."

He looked at her in the unique way he had that always alerted her to an oncoming question or admonition. Big brother stuff he used to pull when she'd gotten herself into trouble and her daddy threatened to send her to boarding school. Sometimes she wished she'd gone. Things would be a lot different now if she had.

She picked up a potato chip. "Want one?"

He shook his head. "Nope. But I do want some answers to a couple of questions."

Studying him intently, she watched his gaze darken and let a deep sigh slide out. "I guessed as much."

Concern crossed his bruised face, but she found herself searching for a deeper meaning in his troubled look. Something to explain the high-powered emotions they'd shared in that one unforgettable night. The night when she realized she wanted Buddy Lee as more than a friend.

"What do you want to know?" Certain now that when he learned the truth that special moment would never be repeated, Faith turned her head to hide her humiliation...and remorse.

Chapter Ten

"I heard what the doctor said, you know." Buddy Lee shifted from one foot to the other. Crossed and uncrossed his arms, finally letting them dangle at his sides.

Faith's eyes widened. "What did you hear?"

"Something about the fact that you'd had similar bruises before today. And that this wasn't the first time Royce had slapped you around. Doc wasn't exactly whispering, you know."

He dragged his hand through his hair. His dark eyes filled with concern. "Truth is, while he was waiting for his nurse Doc told me about the last time this happened."

The anxiety in his voice softened her heart. She wanted to embrace him, to thank him for caring, but she was ashamed of her inadequacy—the weakness that had prompted her to believe whatever Royce had wanted her to believe.

"For cryin' out loud, Faith, how could you let him get away with stuff like that? You should've told me about him right from the start."

His anxiety turned to accusation and she shrank back in the bed. "It wasn't like you think. It only happened once before I came to you for help. And I left when he turned nasty."

Buddy Lee's throat worked and the muscles in his jaw tightened. His eyes grew cold and distant. "But, why wouldn't you trust me with the whole truth? Were you afraid I'd refuse? Was that it? I thought you knew me better than that."

His words were raw with emotion, ragged shards that sliced through her guilt with ruthless abandon. She had hurt him without realizing it. Without meaning to.

"It wasn't like you think." She wanted to explain, but his pained look of disappointment silenced her.

"I don't get it, Faith. I just don't get it." With a shake of his head, he strode from the room.

The anguish in his departing words made her heart ache unbearably with the knowledge that he believed she'd betrayed him. Just like so many other times in her life, she kept disappointing the ones she cared about. Daddy, Mama, and now, Buddy Lee. She choked back a sob. Why couldn't just one thing she did turn out right?

She carried her plate to the kitchen, put away the left-over chicken, and closed the bag of chips with a plastic clip.

Cold fingers of loneliness coiled around her heart. This feeling of desolation was something she'd never experienced before. Buddy Lee had always been there. Even after she'd admitted her mistake with Royce and stood up to her daddy about marrying Buddy Lee, she'd relied on his strength and support. Or had she only imagined his willingness to stand by her? His anger was painful for her to deal with, but the disappointment in his eyes was devastating. She'd never expected that.

Too confused and unsettled by her inner turmoil to go back to bed, she prowled around the tiny living room. A stack of mail carelessly tossed on the end table caught her eye, and she stopped to straighten it.

A thick, cream-colored envelope lay open on the top of the pile. She recognized the local bank's logo. When she picked it up, a single piece of paper fluttered to the floor. She bent to retrieve it.

And gasped when she glanced through the missive. A quote for the purchase of the Mustang! *This can't be right.* Buddy Lee would never sell his beloved car. She knew how much he prized the automobile.

Faith retreated to the sofa and spread the letter across her lap. Spotting another piece of paper in the envelope, she took it out and realized it was from the bank. Suddenly, everything was crystal clear. Daddy had found a way to call in the balance of Buddy Lee's note, using some obscure legality buried in the original loan agreement. With the payment due by the end of the week, Buddy Lee must have decided to sell his car in order to keep from losing his shop.

Angry tears stung her eyes. Her stupid mistake had snowballed, and now her best friend was going to lose everything he'd worked for. No wonder he didn't trust her. She'd ruined his life with her selfishness, insisting that he marry her. Help her out of a mess one more time. A mess of her own making that could've been prevented if she hadn't been in such a hurry to get married and have a family of her own.

Well, she was going to have her family, all right, but at what price? She had no right to expect Buddy Lee to accept Royce's baby as his own. No right at all.

Stuffing the letters back into the envelope, she left them on the end table and went to the bedroom closet to retrieve her suitcase. Somehow, she had to make things right.

The afternoon sun sifted through the dirt-smudged windows of his repair shop and bounced off the glossy surface of Buddy Lee's own private treasure. He stared wistfully at the shiny red Mustang as he wiped an imaginary speck of dust from the hood. Damn, he loved this car. The thought of having to sell it tore his guts right out, but there was no way in hell to come up with enough money to pay off his loan unless he did just that.

He knew when he sold the car there should be enough left over after paying the bank to take decent care of Faith and the baby. Classic cars like this one were worth a small fortune to the right car buff. Celebrities especially liked owning them.

It wasn't like he hadn't planned to sell it some day. He just wasn't ready to sell the sweet thing yet. His dream of becoming well-known for his expertise in the field of restoring these automotive treasures was fading fast. He'd intended to use the Mustang to advertise his craft to major collectors around the country and eventually develop a well-paying career. Then he'd never have to answer to "Boyd's boy" again.

The beginning of a headache throbbed behind his eyes. So much for pipe-dreams. *Deal with it, Walker. You've done it before and you can do it now.* Somehow, his inner pep talk didn't make him feel any better.

He flipped through the current buyers catalog to a page he'd dog-eared earlier. The one offer he'd already received had been lower than he'd wanted, so he'd declined. He wasn't giving the car away, for cryin' out loud.

There were a couple of collectors in the Galveston area who might meet his asking price. He'd heard of them through a contact in Houston. Lots of good money down on the Gulf Coast. He'd often thought of relocating to that area. Sun, sand, surf, and plenty of eager clients with money to burn. Yessir, that would be a perfect set-up for his dream business.

A derisive laugh slipped out. No more dreams for him. Being responsible for Faith and her child was a reality check guaranteed to put the skids on any of those fantasies damn straight. But he wouldn't have it any other way.

Knowing he couldn't put it off any longer, he went into his office and picked up the phone, but before he had time to dial, a rough voice behind him cut through the dial tone in his ear.

"Nice car, Walker."

Buddy Lee slammed the phone down and spun around, knocking over a half-empty cup of stale coffee in his haste. He tossed a shop rag over the mess and uttered a graphic word he didn't use very often.

The last man he ever wanted to see again stood in the doorway with a nasty smirk distorting his swollen lip and bruised face. Living proof that slime could walk and talk.

He bolted out of his office to bar the way to the work area, primed and ready to go head-to-head if necessary. "What the hell are you doing here, Webb? If you aim to walk out of here upright, you've got five seconds to haul ass and that's being generous." He itched for an excuse to permanently rearrange Royce's face.

Royce remained near the entry door. "Well now," he said, his smirk turning into an ugly leer, "I've got some interesting information I think you'll want to hear."

"You've got nothing to say that's worth my attention," Buddy Lee snapped. His whole his body tightened. How could Faith have ever imagined she was in love with this worthless piece of garbage?

"Oh, no? Well, listen to this." Royce moved ever so slightly inside the door and lowered his voice to a hoarse whisper. "I know the baby isn't yours, Walker." He snickered. "Did you really think I wouldn't find out about your little scheme? You did well for yourself, marrying Faith and claiming my child. Especially with your small-time business about to go belly-up."

"What do you mean?" Buddy Lee lunged, but Royce was too quick. He side-stepped just out of reach.

"Oh, I know all about your note and the sorry state of your bank account. Don't forget, I work at the bank. All sorts of information crosses my desk. I'm sure you don't want Faith's daddy to find out who the baby's *real* father is, now do you? That would ruin your little scheme to get your hands on Faith's money." His eyes glittered like a predator closing in on a kill. "But, I'll keep my mouth shut for a price."

The nasty threat turned Buddy Lee's blood to ice water. Did Royce really know the truth or was he just bluffing? Doc

Sutter was the only other person who knew that privileged information.

"You're crazier than I thought, Webb, if you believe that," he snarled. "You don't have any proof."

"Oh, I've got proof, all right. And don't think I won't use it. Ever heard of DNA? No court in Texas would deny me the right to my own child. Faith would have to agree to share custody. And wouldn't that just please old man Morgan? The kid wouldn't have the disgrace of being a Walker, after all." Royce edged toward the door with all the stealth of a coward.

Buddy Lee winced. What Royce said was true. The Walker name didn't come with any social clout or fancy family tree. But what it did come with was his own sense of honor and decency. If push came to shove, he'd deal with the Devil himself, just so Faith could stay with him.

The hole in his heart got bigger. He'd made a promise to her. What kind of sorry excuse for a friend would he be if he failed? *Loser, loser, loser.* Just like his daddy.

"So, do you want that kid or not?" Royce prodded.

Did he? Could he honestly say "yes"? His gut knotted as he wrestled with his conscience, wondering what else was on the man's twisted mind.

"What's it to you?" He balled his fists at his side. Every time he moved, the sharp pain under his ribs reminded him he'd be better off to avoid another brawl. *Dammit.*

"You have something I want," Royce said. "Take me up on my offer and I'm out of your hair for good. No one will hear the truth about the kid from me—ever. Let the little ankle-biter make *your* life miserable. I never wanted any part of parenthood."

"I'm listening." Buddy Lee clenched and unclenched his fists to keep from smashing Webb's face. The man wasn't worthy of breathing the same air as Faith. How could she have wanted to marry him?

"Give me your Mustang, free and clear. That's a real easy way for you to keep Faith and her sprout, eh?" He glanced at his watch. "It's two o'clock now. Plenty of time for you to get the title transferred. But, if you don't, just remember, I've got proof. Would you want to drag Faith through all that and take a chance that she'd change her mind and marry me after all, for the sake of the child?"

Royce rubbed the bruised side of his face, then his mouth twisted in a sinister smirk. "I'll be back tonight after you close up. Deal?"

Buddy Lee's mind was spinning U-ees again. Faith or his livelihood? He would lose, no matter which one he chose.

"Let me get this straight. You want my car in return for giving up your claim as the father of Faith's child? What kind of pond scum are you, anyway? And why should I trust you?"

"Life's full of unexpected hazards, Walker. I've already figured out what's important to me. Now you'll have to decide what's more important to you, your business or Faith and her brat."

"What guarantee do I have that you'll keep quiet after you have the car? That you won't show up later to claim the child?"

"You'll just have to trust me, won't you?"

"Like that's gonna happen," Buddy Lee scoffed. As far as he was concerned, the words *trust* and *honor* weren't used in the same breath as Royce Webb's name. He didn't trust a dead snake anymore than a live one. Webb definitely qualified for one of the two.

"Believe me, I'll be far away from this two-bit town. You and Faithwill be the first things I'll forget." He tossed Buddy Lee an arrogant salute. "Have the car ready to roll when I come back."

Buddy Lee reined in his fury and waited a full ten seconds before he slammed the door on Webb's retreating back. If he hadn't, Deputy Pike and his men would've had one helluva homicide to clean up.

Charging back into the work area, he grabbed a wrench and hurled it against the wall. That should've made him feel better, but it didn't. He was so damned mad, he slung the protective canvas over the Mustang before he accidentally did permanent damage to it. Then he yanked open the hood of Joe Bob's delivery truck and peered in, but he couldn't remember what the heck he was supposed to fix.

"So, Walker, whaddaya' hear from the sheriff? They ever figure out if somebody was in the shop or not?"

Without warning, a gravelly voice close to his ear jarred Buddy Lee from his deep concentration. He whipped around sudden-like and thwacked his head a good one on the underside of the truck hood. *Sonuva...!*

"Dammit, Scooter, how many times have I told you not to sneak up on me when I'm working?" He could feel a lump already taking shape when he rubbed his hand over the injured spot. Cripes! What else?

"Yeah, I know, B.L., I just forgot. Sorry, dude." Scooter sent Buddy Lee a remorseful glance, set his can of cola on the cluttered workbench and slouched against the truck fender.

"Well, try to remember, okay? And no, Elroy hasn't figured out a damn thing." The throbbing in his head increased.

"Too bad. But, hey, what I come by to tell you is...I saw that same gorilla-looking fella again yesterday, driving out by the county line. I was walking back from a card game at Homer Seavers' place and that goon shot past me doin' eighty, at least. Durn near hit me, too. Dumb dipstick."

"That right?" Buddy Lee tried not to show too much interest, which wasn't hard to do since the granddaddy of all headaches was making his eyes start to cross.

With Scooter latching on to every bit of hearsay like a leech on bare skin, Buddy Lee didn't want to encourage his participation in this particular situation. Not yet, anyway. But he wasn't against getting a little information of his own.

"What time was that?" He tried massaging his temples. No relief there.

"Oh, must've been gettin' on towards dark-thirty. I was hurrying to get home in time to watch that new fishing show on the cable channel, ya' know? Nearly nine, I reckon. Lost my watch, so I ain't for sure. Why?"

Why. Scooter's aggravating, all-time favorite word. "No reason." He was really straining now to keep from swearing a blue streak at the pain in his head. "Did you happen to notice which way he went when he got to I-35?"

"Yep, headed South. Probably going to San Antone." Scooter shrugged and retrieved his drink. One last swallow finished it off, then he tossed the can in the recycle bin and dragged his sleeve across his mouth. "By the way, how come your face looks like you walked into a swinging door? Married life gettin' the best of you?" He guffawed and pretended to punch Buddy Lee's arm.

Buddy Lee glared at him. "My married life is fine." *Yeah, it just keeps getting better and better.* But at least he was getting used to sleeping on the sofa. He could go a full two hours now before he had to get up and walk the kinks out of his back. Something to celebrate, right along with his celibate life-style and lack of a healthy bank account. Sheese!

Scooter angled him a doubtful look. "So how'd you get the bruises then?"

"Well, I sure as hell didn't get them from my wife." He stomped over to the vending machine and shoved some quarters in the slot.

From the corner of his eye, he could see Scooter pacing back and forth. His friend's impatience wasn't hard to miss, but if he was waiting to find out the rest of the story, tough luck. Wasn't gonna happen.

"Speaking of Faith," Scooter prompted, a slow grin hitching up the corners of his mouth, "how's she getting along? Sure lots of folks curious about what's happened. You know, 'bout the baby and stuff."

"Why would they be curious about that?" Buddy Lee pulled back the tab on his can of root beer. "Nothing happened that they didn't learn about in Mr. Garvey's biology class."

He took a long, deep swallow. Something Scooter had mentioned about seeing that shady character in Liberty again bothered the hell out of him. Nagged like a sore tooth. Shoot, he sure didn't need anything more to worry about.

"Well," Scooter stuck his hand in the plastic jar behind a red tool box and pulled out a licorice whip from Buddy Lee's private stash. Two bites later, he said, "There's talk that Royce has been asking some questions around town about the two of you. And Faith's daddy let it be known that he and the missus didn't approve of their daughter carrying on with you at all."

Buddy Lee swore under his breath. "Like the whole town didn't already know *that*. What else are they saying?"

Scooter went for another licorice whip. "Some are wonderin' if Faith's gonna go to Doc Sutter. You know, for the baby and all. MayBeth Patterson heard from a neighbor that Faith had already called some doctor in Granite City. And some folks are even wonderin' if she's really having a baby, 'cause she don't even look like she's three months gone. You know. Just stuff like that." He bit off more licorice and chewed noisily.

"Hellfire, Scoot, has anyone in this town thought about minding their own business? Faith is doing just fine and so am I, thank you very much." Buddy Lee slammed his cold drink can on top of his tool box. "Pass it on," he muttered right before he slid under the truck on a grease-coated creeper.

He grabbed the first wrench he saw and attacked a rusty bolt with a vengeance. Why was he surprised that he and Faith were the hot topic of gossip around town? He'd more or less expected that. What worried him the most was the ultimatum Royce had given him. How the hell could he *not* choose Faith and the baby? But if he did, how would he support them if he lost the shop? Which he surely would with no money. His headache now reached the intensity of a dozen out-of-control jackhammers.

He pounded at the stubborn bolt, missed and smacked his thumb. He swore. Very loudly. Very colorfully.

"Well, hell, don't get your boxers in a bunch, B.L.," Scooter said. "I was just answerin' your questions. What's got you so riled, anyway?"

He just grunted "Hummph" and kept on working. Maybe if he ignored him, his friend would go away.

Scooter leaned down to peer under the truck. His head bumped the fender, throwing him off balance. When he shuffled to keep from falling, his foot plowed into a pile of tools. The entire thirty-six-piece set of wrenches and screwdrivers flew across the floor, along with a brand-new set of sockets he'd managed to knock off the fender.

Buddy Lee shot out from under the truck like the creeper was powered by a V-8 engine.

"Dammit, Scooter, don't you have some place to be?"

Liberty's number one connection to the Gossip Channel looked down at him with eyes lit up like he'd just had an epiphany. "You ain't gettin' any, are you, B.L?" He slapped his knee and cackled. "No wonder you're so testy."

Buddy Lee chunked an empty oil can at his friend, hating like hell when Scooter was right. "Not that it matters," he muttered. There were other problems to consider besides his desire to take Faith to bed again.

Scooter hustled out the door and down the street, still laughing.

Buddy Lee crawled back under the truck. With luck, and a whole lot of concentration, he should be able to focus on those problems any minute now.

An hour later, he flipped the CLOSED sign on the door and went home. He still didn't know what was wrong with Joe Bob's truck, but he'd figured out what to do about Faith.

Chapter Eleven

"**Y**ou're early." Faith turned from where she stood at the kitchen sink, a dish towel in her hand.

Buddy Lee glanced at the dishes in the soapy water, then back at her. Shadows lurked beneath her eyes and her face was drawn, fatigue evident in the fine lines pinching the corners of her mouth. His heart lurched right before his protective mode kicked in. He almost forgot how angry he'd been when he'd stormed out earlier.

"Shouldn't you be resting? You don't have to do the housework around here. I can take care of it." He tried to tame the edge of roughness in his voice, but couldn't, no matter how hard he tried.

They'd parted on a sour note and he ought to apologize, but he was still smarting from the fact that he'd pretty much given her his blind trust when he married her and yet, she hadn't trusted him enough to tell him the whole truth about her relationship with Royce. About his abusive nature. That was a whole lot to swallow, but he was trying.

She took a hesitant step forward. Offered him a half-smile, then said with a slight shrug of her shoulders. "I didn't do much. Washing a few dishes won't hurt me."

"Yeah, well...." How much was too much? What he knew about expectant mamas you could put in one of those fancy tea cups with room left over, but he was pretty sure they needed a lot of rest. Especially when they'd been roughed up like Faith had been. If he was feeling like he'd been dragged through a knot-hole backwards, he could just imagine how she felt.

She looked so small and fragile. He knew she liked to put on a tough front, one he'd seen up close more than once, but today she appeared especially vulnerable. And he felt so damned helpless about the whole mess.

"Buddy Lee...." She placed her hand on his arm.

"Faith, I...." The electric shock of her touch jolted him and his words bumped into hers.

She looked up at him, green eyes soft and shining. "I'm sorry about this morning." Her small hand slid down to burrow its way into his big one. "I know I should've told you about the other time, about Royce and all, but I was ashamed. Everything was so mixed up. I couldn't ask any more of you. Believe me, I never thought...." Her voice wobbled. She turned away and hurried out of the room, but not before he saw tears dampen her cheeks.

He found her standing in his bedroom, staring out the window, arms crossed protectively at her waist. Her suitcase lay open on the bed, the clothes she'd taken on their honeymoon neatly arranged inside.

I'm losing her. His heart dropped so suddenly, his nervous system short-circuited.

There was nothing he could do to stop her from leaving if she really wanted to. And giving up the Mustang in exchange for

Royce's silence wasn't going to do a damn bit of good. Losing the shop was imminent but no longer important. His life would be a big fat zero without Faith in it. His heart slowly broke into a million tiny pieces.

Unsure what to say, he approached her quietly, resting his hands lightly on her shoulders and hoping desperately that she wouldn't push him away. She stiffened beneath his touch but he kept his hands where they were. His mouth was dry, like he'd sucked up all the sand along the Gulf Coast and forgotten to spit it out. When he spoke, the rawness in his throat made his voice gritty and coarse.

"Don't go, Faith. Please." He dared to draw her back against him and bury his face in her hair. "I'm sorry," he breathed against her ear. "I'm so sorry."

She turned in his arms, looked at him with eyes still sparkling with tears. He reached up to brush one that was caught at the corner of her mouth.

"You'll be safer with me gone, Buddy. Look what a mess I've made of everything. If I'm not around, Royce will leave you alone. I'll go where he can't find me. It will be better for both of us." She looked away. "I never meant to bring you harm."

"Aw, Faith, don't you think I know that? I wouldn't have married you if I'd thought of you that way."

Wanting her to know he spoke the truth, and because he wanted to watch her reaction when he finally told her, he tipped her face so she could look into his eyes. Then gulped a deep give-me-strength breath. "I married you because I wanted to. Because I–"

"You never would've done it if I hadn't begged you."

He'd almost admitted he loved her, but now the words stuck in his throat. "Maybe not, but I did, and that's all that matters. Stay, Faith. Let me take care of you." His mouth a whisper away from hers. "Please," he murmured against her lips.

Faith's pulse danced wildly. Wrapped in the circle of Buddy Lee's arms was the only place she wanted to be, but she hadn't dared to believe he might feel the same. Not after the way she'd hidden the truth about Royce's earlier abuse.

She had no right to expect him to trust her, let alone love her. He hadn't said he loved her, but, oh, how she longed for it. This man, her wonderful, life-long hero, had turned out to be the one she loved with all her heart, yet there was no way she could right the wrongs she'd caused, except by leaving him.

His mouth came down on hers with a whispered plea just then and all rational thought flew out the window, leaving her with only the aching need to be with Buddy Lee one last time.

She slid her arms around his neck and tunneled her fingers through his thick, coffee-dark hair. Raised up on her tiptoes so she could deepen the kiss. When he groaned and explored her mouth with his tongue, the heat of her own desire throbbed low between her thighs.

"Yes, Buddy Lee," she murmured, when the kiss finally broke. "Yes."

In an instant, she was swept up in his arms and carried to the bed as tenderly and carefully as he might have carried a china doll. But this time, the hurt she felt was the one in her heart for causing him pain. This time, she wanted to love him enough to make him love her back, if only for a little while. Just long enough to make a memory to hold in her heart. She closed her eyes as he laid her on the bed and stretched out beside her.

"Faith," he whispered, "look at me."

She did, and his dark eyes were filled with such tenderness and passion, the ache in her heart spread to every thrumming part of her body.

He cupped her chin, placed a kiss on the tip of her nose. "I want to love you slow and sweet this time, darlin'."

He feathered kisses down the smooth column of her neck while his hands slipped under her blouse and gathered her breasts, kneading them gently.

She sighed. Melted back into the bed and gave herself up to the pleasure, and the wonder, of his touch.

With almost no effort, he removed her blouse, unhooked her bra. Both garments landed in a heap on the floor. Her shorts and panties followed.

His hands never left her body, touching, caressing, enticing. His mouth followed his hands, exploring, tasting, exciting. Every nerve ending screamed for help. Every sensitized inch of her body begged for more. So did she.

Magically, his own clothes joined hers, and when he moved over her with such tenderness, she felt fragile and treasured. And loved.

"Ahhh," he murmured, when their bodies touched.

"Ohhh," she sighed, when he slid one leg between hers and the friction sent a current of electricity surging through her.

He dedicated his attention to the welfare of her breasts, loving each one slowly, dividing his time between them so that when his mouth was exquisitely busy with one, the other felt bereaved. Whimpering with need, she brought his hand to the lonely one.

He moved slowly, next focusing on her lower belly and its quivering softness. Never had she been so physically aware of her own body, the curves and hollows that he nuzzled and kissed.

Heated passion threatened to devour her with its flames. Buddy Lee had awakened her to pleasure, but more than that, he'd awakened her to honest-to-goodness love and the sharp, sweet thrill of it took her breath away.

She arched her body, needing his closeness. The fullness of his arousal pressed against her thigh and she opened her legs.

His mouth found its way back to hers and he kissed her gently, sweetly. And not nearly enough. She deepened the kiss, her tongue stroking and teasing until he growled deep in his throat.

With one hand, she circled him, moving deliberately until she felt his response. Then she guided him to her, amazed at the way their bodies melted into one. Her heart filled with a love deeper than she'd imagined possible, for now she knew that Buddy Lee had sacrificed everything he held dear because he loved her.

She wanted to give love back to him for the same reason. How blind she'd been not to see that he'd been right there all those years, waiting for her to love him. Now she intended to make up for lost time. How could she have missed what her heart had known all along?

"Whatever happens, I'll always love you, Buddy Lee," she whispered, desire and need thickening her voice.

Buddy Lee's blood roared in his ears so loud he could barely hear above the pounding. *She loved him? Was it possible?* But when he looked down at her face all soft and dewy, eagerness shining in her sea-green eyes, he knew. Oh, yeah, he knew.   Unbelievable as it was, his beautiful wife loved him. Not just as a means of keeping her child. Definitely not for his name, though that had come with the marriage. No, she had said she loved *him*, Buddy Lee Walker. He'd been carrying around a heart overloaded with love for so long, it finally burst through like a river overflowing its banks.

He wanted to shout his good fortune to the heavens, to the whole world, and especially to every Liberty, Texas busybody who ever called him *Boyd's boy*. But he didn't. Nope. Right now, this precious moment belonged to them, and he wasn't about to share it with anyone.

"I've always loved you, darlin'." His mouth was close to hers, lips almost touching, hearts beating as one. "And no matter what happens, I'll take care of you." He brushed her lips with the softest of kisses.

He'd promised her slow and sweet, but every time he tried to slow the pace, Faith took the initiative and left him balancing precariously on the edge of Paradise. An incredible place to be, where a man could die from sheer ecstasy. He fought to control the age-old force that drove them both closer to the precipice.

"Faith, my sweet Faith," he urged against her mouth, "hold on to the moment, darlin'. Hold on to me."

And she did. Dug her fingernails into his shoulders, kissed him hot and wet and deep. No holds barred.

Together, they flew through the heavens, then tumbled through space on the same wild, sweeping storm of passion.

Eventually, she stirred in his arms, and Buddy Lee took pleasure in watching her as she uncurled and stretched her warm, sweet body. He gave in to the urge to kiss her awake.

Her sleepy, sexy response triggered an answer from his own eager body, and he longed to satisfy them both one more time, but any further plan for a leisurely repeat performance came to a screeching halt when he remembered other unfinished business. His Mustang...and Royce.

"Promise me you'll be here when I get back," he murmured into her mouth as he drew back from the kiss.

His body hummed with need when she rubbed her lips against his chest, nipped at his skin, then snuggled into the curve of his arm and aligned her body with his. Sweet heaven, he wanted to stay right where he was forever. Plus a couple of extra days, if it could be arranged.

"Mmmm," she crooned and reached for him. "I'll be here."

He closed his eyes and moved over her once more, unable to resist. The world and all its woes were forgotten for a little while longer.

An hour later, he slipped quietly from the room, reluctant to disturb her sleep. But he left his heart with her. Right where it belonged.

"Call the cops, Walker!" Scooter slam-banged through the front of Buddy Lee's shop, jerking the door open and hollering at the top of his smoke-ravaged lungs. "B.L., get the hell out here, will you? I just saw your 'stang goin' down the street. Call Elroy!"

Buddy Lee emerged from the work area, wiping his hands on a polishing rag. "Knock it off, Scoot. I don't need Elroy or any of his badges poking around here." He tossed the rag into a nearby cardboard box.

"But...but, your car. Somebody was headin' out of town with it. I swear!" Behind his black-rimmed glasses, Scooter's eyes were bigger than a hoot owl's.

Buddy Lee wondered if there was a sign on his back that said "Dump All Bad Luck Here." He was sure collecting a heap. He'd hoped, after surrendering his automobile tonight, right along with a portion of his soul, that Royce wouldn't be spotted when he left the garage. Everybody and their uncle could recognize his Mustang a mile away, even after dark. Wouldn't you know Scooter'd be the one person in the entire town to show up just as his beloved car wheeled out of town? Shoot and damn!

"Sit down, Scooter. Catch your breath before you pass out."

Buddy Lee pointed to a metal folding chair propped against the wall. He took the battered swivel office chair for himself, settled in for what he knew was going to be a barrage of questions.

While Scooter was struggling to find his breath and his voice, Buddy Lee tried to figure out just how much, if anything, he should tell his friend. Next to nothing was preferable, but not probable, he feared.

Scooter made a big to-do of unfolding the rusty chair and sitting down. He took off his gimme cap and scratched his head.

"I cain't believe you aren't gonna call Elroy." He raised an eyebrow at Buddy Lee, his eyes full of questions. "You been hittin' the brew or something?"

"No, I'm not drinking and I don't plan on calling Elroy." He ducked his head and stared at his shoes. "The Mustang has a new owner, that's all," he mumbled.

"The hell you say!" Scooter shot up off the chair like he'd been jabbed in the butt with a cattle prod. "You gotta be on drugs."

Buddy Lee shook his head. Doggone, he was gonna wind up spilling the whole story to Scooter after all, just to keep him from blabbing what he'd seen all over town.

He huffed out a deep sigh. "Sit down, Scoot, and I'll try to explain."

"Well, I sure as hell hope so." Scooter prowled around until he located the plastic container of licorice whips Buddy Lee had shoved under the counter. He grabbed a handful and slouched back in the chair.

"Okay, dude, let's have it. From the beginning." He chewed thoughtfully and gave Buddy Lee his rapt attention.

Twenty minutes and a whole lot of explaining and cussing later, Buddy Lee got up to fetch cold drinks for the two of them, leaving his friend shaking his head in wonder and total confusion.

"You got any money at all, B.L.?" Scooter's voice was low, almost reverent. "How you gonna pay your bills?"

How, indeed? Buddy Lee wondered, and swallowed down the taste of failure creeping up the back of his throat.

"No money," he admitted, "not enough, anyway, and no hope of getting any more." He cleared his throat. "Guess I'll lose the shop. I can always get a job fixing cars at a dealership in Granite City, I suppose."

"Hey, man, rotten luck." Scooter got up and gave his friend an awkward pat on the back. "What're you gonna do about Faith?"

"Meaning?"

"You know, how're you gonna support a wife? You ain't gonna have two nickels to rub together for a while. And babies cost a helluva lot, I hear."

Buddy Lee frowned. Scooter's habit of raining on parades was about as much fun as a slap upside the head. Jeez. "Faith is *not* to find out about this, understand? Not one word. I'll figure out something. The main thing is to keep Royce from showing up and trying to claim the baby. He'll stop at nothing to get revenge, if he's of a mind to. As far as this town knows, Scoot, the baby's mine. That's the way Faith wants it, hear? Not even her folks know any different. And nobody but Doc Sutter, and now you, know the whole story."

He walked over to Scooter and placed a firm hand on his shoulder. "I'm counting on you to see that it stays that way."

Scooter nodded. "You know I can keep a secret, B.L.."

"Yeah, well--" Buddy Lee had his own opinion on that, but he had to trust his friend this time. What other choice was there?

It was after eleven when he finally left the shop. Faith would be worried, but he didn't call. Didn't want to wake her. Thinking of how he'd left her in his bed, so warm and well-loved, he knew he'd done the right thing by relinquishing his valuable Mustang to Royce. Making certain there was no longer any threat to Faith or her child was all he wanted. Keeping Royce Webb out of their lives permanently would always be his priority.

Pretty sure that Scooter would keep the details of the sordid mess to himself, Buddy Lee stayed in his office, going over the books, looking at every possible way to scrape enough money together to pay his note. There wasn't any. He'd known that even before he started searching. Still he'd hoped.

He rested his head in his hands and grudgingly accepted the fact that there was still one last possibility. A choice he'd tried his best to avoid, but now he had to swallow his pride and go for it. For Faith.

"Are you sure he gave the car to Royce, Scooter?" Faith sat at the little kitchen table trying to make sense out of what Buddy Lee's friend had just told her.

Startled out of a sound sleep by a frantic knock at the door, she had stumbled out of bed to find Scooter in such a state of distress he'd babbled incoherently until she let him in. Now he sat across from her at the table, fidgeting and darting glances around the room.

Faith wondered if he'd been drinking. Scooter's wild story about Buddy Lee giving his Mustang away to Royce was just too unbelievable. He'd never do that. Especially when she knew he needed the money and intended to sell it.

"God's truth, Faith," Scooter swore, crossing his heart and placing his hand on his chest in a child-like gesture. "I figured you oughta know about it, even though I promised B.L. I wouldn't say nothing. He'll probably have my hide if he ever finds out. But, dammit all, that car was his ace-in-the-hole. Kinda a safety net, ya' know, and now he's gone and lost it to that scumbag, Webb. He wouldn't do a dang fool thing like that unless he had good reason. He's got nothin' left. It ain't fair, Faith. Buddy Lee never hurt nobody in his whole life." He fiddled with the cold drink on the table in front of him.

She'd given him a glass of iced tea when he first sat down. She wasn't about to offer him anything stronger, even if he wasn't driving. He was already bouncing off the walls.

After listening to his story, her whole body shook with anger. At Royce, for the degrading way he'd used and abused her; at her father, for putting the importance of money before his family; and at her mother, for allowing it. But most of all, she was angry with herself for the tangled mess she'd made of her life...and Buddy Lee's.

Leaving him wasn't the answer. That was too much like running away. She needed to be here for him, the same way he'd stood by her so many times. Yes, this time she would do what had to be done.

"I'm glad you told me, Scooter. You did the right thing. And don't worry, I'll make sure Buddy Lee doesn't find out."

"An' you did the right thing, too, marrying him instead of Royce," Scooter said, nodding emphatically.

That was true. She'd realized it the minute she found the evidence of Buddy Lee's intention to sell the car. That had been hard enough to accept. But the impact of knowing he'd given it away, sacrificed it for her in order to keep Royce from claiming her child and complicating her life, simply overwhelmed her.

Buddy Lee had tried to keep her safe, like he'd always done. And he'd shown his love for her in so many ways. Ways that, as a defiant, self-absorbed teen, she hadn't recognized. Thank God, she'd finally grown up enough to see what was in her heart. She loved him, too, and this new discovery was all that mattered now.

She sat at the table for a long time after Scooter left, sorting through the events of the last few weeks. What had driven her to accept Royce's proposal in the first place? Their relationship had never come close to what she had now. Oh, he'd been attentive, showered her with compliments and took her to all the right places on dates, but none of that had given her an inner joy. Something had been missing, but she'd chosen not to search for it.

Looking back now, she realized Royce had always been distant. Even the one time they made love, he'd been too insistent, too forceful. There'd been no romance except in her imagination. How had she missed that? Had she really believed her father's approval of Royce Webb validated her choice? Hoped her choice would make him proud? If so, she'd been dead wrong.

All she'd accomplished was to make matters worse. Her recent actions had changed the course of both her own life and Buddy Lee's. Even her parents' lives had been affected by what she'd done. And how typical that she'd shocked and embarrassed them again. In her own selfish desire to prove her personal worth to her father, to make him sit up and take notice of her, she'd managed to put lives in danger, destroying any respect she might have gained.

And how typical that Buddy Lee had come to her rescue once more. She didn't deserve to have him in her life, but knowing he was there made her heart swell with emotions too immense to contain. He deserved all the love she had to give. All she had to do now was convince him to accept what she offered.

The clock on the bedside table glowed eerily in the room's darkness when she finally crawled back into bed to wait for her husband to come home. One-fifteen. Where was he?

Chapter Twelve

There were no lights on in the Morgan mansion when Buddy Lee stopped his truck at the front entrance and got out. A full five minutes passed before the man of the house answered the door and another five before he agreed to let his son-in-law in.

"What makes you think I'll help you, Walker?" Lionel Morgan sat behind his desk, studying the tip of his imported cigar as he spoke. With slow, precise movements, he snipped the end off with a gold clipper, touched a flame to it from a matching gold lighter in the shape of a dollar sign, and puffed a couple of times to draw the fire.

Buddy Lee stood in front of the massive mahogany desk, aware that he was seeing the banker at his pompous best, but dammit, he refused to be intimidated by his father-in-law's air of superiority.

A ribbon of pungent cigar smoke curled toward him, stung his nostrils and made his eyes water, but he stayed where he was and stubbornly refused to cough. Instead, he silently choked back a string of colorful suggestions as to what the man could do with his gawdawful habit, and took satisfaction in the sour look pinching Lionel's mouth.

The banker leaned back in his leather chair with such a high-and-mighty expression, Buddy Lee had to ball his hands into fists to keep from punching him right between the eyes. Of course, that would only make matters worse and add another alligator to his already overstocked swamp.

"Thought you might want to do it for Faith," he said, keeping a tight lock on his emotions, in spite of the slow burn spreading through him.

There was no sound in the house other than the ticking of the carved grandfather clock in the hall. When it chimed the last of twelve notes, his glance shifted to the window. Already midnight. Liberty's inhabitants were likely tucked in bed by now, safe and sound, oblivious to what was taking place inside the Morgan residence.

He wished now he'd phoned Faith from the shop. He hadn't intended to be gone this late. If she was still awake, she'd be worried as all get-out and the last thing she needed from him was more grief. One of these days, he'd see about getting a cellular phone, so when her time got closer she could get in touch with him no matter where he was. But for now, he'd be damned if he'd ask her daddy for any more favors. Not even the use of his phone.

Lionel snorted. "Faith gave up her family when she took up with the likes of you. Her mother and I no longer consider her our daughter."

He thought he heard a twinge of regret in the old man's voice, but he'd swiveled around in his chair so that all Buddy Lee could see was his back. And everyone knew Lionel Morgan didn't waste time on regrets.

A fist of bitterness clenched his gut. Morgan didn't deserve to have a daughter as fine as Faith. By God, neither did Beryl. She'd been a shadow of her husband for too many years, never standing up for Faith when Lionel bad-mouthed her in public. Faith had never had the mama she needed. His heart twitched at that thought. His own mama had been a loving one, but he hadn't had her nearly long enough.

He remembered how Lionel's public reprimands had humiliated Faith something awful. She'd pretended not to care, but her thinly disguised hurt was obvious. And his heart had broken for her because he loved her and he couldn't take away her pain. That's when he hated his name most of all. *Boyd's boy* would never be good enough for a Morgan.

"You know, you're no better than my old man," Buddy Lee spat out. "He didn't give a damn about his kid, either. But guess what? Your money didn't make you a good parent. You should've paid attention to your daughter long before this. Why the hell do you think she pulled those crazy stunts when she was younger?"

He planted both hands on the desk and aimed his words at Lionel's back. "Do you know why she challenged every rule you ever made for her? She wanted your attention, you damned old man, not your money. But you were so blind you drove her away with your demands for perfection. You focused on her faults, instead of her goodness and the qualities that made her the wonderful woman she is. The daughter you should be proud of."

Lionel spun his chair around, stood up and leaned across the desk into Buddy Lee's face. His eyes blazed hot. His scowl was fierce, and when he stabbed the air with his cigar, Buddy Lee dodged sideways to keep from getting branded.

"What goodness?" Lionel's deep voice boomed like thunder. "She shamed her mama and me with her wild ways. She'll bring no more disgrace to this family. When she chose to have your baby and claim the Walker name, she gave up any rights to her heritage." His face contorted with rage as he shook his fist. "And don't forget, your note is still due day after tomorrow. Now get out of this house and don't come back again, begging favors like a loser." He clamped the cigar between his teeth so hard, Buddy Lee expected it to fall apart.

The air between them crackled with resentment. Buddy Lee figured he'd better leave before he did something he'd regret, like leaving the imprint of his fist in the banker's florid face. Damn, it was getting harder and harder to keep from acting like the notorious Boyd's boy. He reeled in his anger with every bit of gut strength he could summon. But he couldn't leave without saying one more thing. He lowered his voice and let the anger heat his words.

"Faith's only shame was the burden of your wealth. She never wanted to be different, but because of you and your blasted money, she believed she was, and she hated that. The real loser is you, Morgan. So, live with that...sir."

On that parting shot, he stormed out, so full of rage he didn't notice Faith's mama standing in the hallway until she spoke.

"Lionel?" she questioned in that soft voice of hers. "Why are you shouting at Buddy Lee?"

He didn't stop, just kept on going. He'd already reached the porch when he heard Lionel answer her.

"Go on back to bed, Beryl. You didn't see anyone, you hear? Not Boyd's boy or anyone else. Now, go."

Well, isn't that the final kick in the ass? He thought as he climbed in his truck. So, Boyd's boy is invisible, huh? He stomped on the accelerator, laid a patch as he peeled out of the drive, and hoped he'd permanently embedded a bitchin' black streak in the fancy driveway.

Not exactly anxious to face his wife and admit he was fixing to lose everything he owned, Buddy Lee drove to the outskirts of town and turned down a deserted gravel road. After making certain there was no one around, he hit the gas pedal, spit a shower of dirt with his wheels and took his truck on a ride that would make any NASCAR driver proud.

After three high-speed passes up and down the road, slinging gravel and cussin' a blue streak, he headed home, no closer to solving his problems, but finally able to face the gnawing fear in his gut.

He had to tell Faith about the car, but not tonight. It was already past one o'clock in the morning. Tonight he needed to hold her close, commit the feel of her to memory, and surround himself with her softness.

Would she leave when she realized she'd married a loser? Would she and the baby be all right without him? Jeez Looeeze! He sure as hell wouldn't be all right without **her**. The precious time he and Faith had spent in each other's arms would soon be only a memory. Could he settle for that? Would he? Not very damned likely.

He'd thought he could, at first. Thought his heart was immune to any more hurt. But that was long before she'd said those three words that turned him inside out, upside down, and every which way but loose. How could he ever go back to loving her only in his dreams?

Faith heard the pounding on the door before Buddy Lee did. She'd awakened sometime during the night to find him lying next to her, but she hadn't bothered to look at the clock. When he'd stirred and flung his arm across her waist, she lay perfectly still, absorbing the warmth of his touch. Lying with her body pressed to his, she sighed and welcomed the delicious sensation created by their closeness. Mmmmm, lovely. She imagined sharing her life with this man who had shown her more love than she deserved.

The pounding grew louder.

She shook his shoulder. "Buddy Lee, someone's at the front door."

He sat up, rubbing his eyes. "What the hell could anyone want at this hour?" He pulled on his jeans, grumbling and stumbling all the way down the hall.

Faith followed, shivering with fear. Had Royce returned? Instinctively, protectively, she crossed her arms over her tummy.

In the living room, Buddy Lee flicked on the small lamp by the sofa before turning on the porch light. Elroy Pike's face stared at him from the other side of the tiny square window in the front door.

Buddy Lee yanked it open. "Elroy, what the...?"

A hot, muggy breeze accompanied the deputy sheriff as he stepped through the threshold. "Gonna have to take you in for questioning, Buddy Lee. Sorry."

The man's apologetic half-shrug didn't quite ring true. He raked a sidelong glance over Faith while he spoke.

She stepped back, aware that Buddy Lee's oversized t-shirt she'd worn to bed barely covered her hips. She tugged at the hem and frowned. Elroy Pike might be related by his marriage to a distant cousin, but she'd never liked him much. Liked him even less now. The sly looks he always managed to aim her way reminded her of a back-alley tomcat on the prowl. Her cousin was more than welcome to him.

"Elroy, why do you need to question Buddy Lee? What's wrong? Did Daddy send you over here?"

The lawman jerked his thumb toward Buddy Lee's unzipped jeans and bare chest. "You'd better get dressed," he said, before turning to Faith. "It's only routine questioning, Faith. Just doing my duty as a deputy of the county." He slid a narrow gaze between them, arched an eyebrow. "Did I interrupt you two from...?"

"Oh, for cryin' out loud, Elroy," Buddy Lee muttered and took off in a trot to fetch a shirt. He was back before Faith could prod Elroy into an argument.

"If it's only routine, then you shouldn't have a problem explaining what it's all about," she demanded.

Buddy Lee came in, tucking his shirt inside his jeans. "Yeah, Elroy, what the hell's so important you had to wake us up in the middle of the night?" He'd stuck his feet into a pair of scuffed running shoes, but left the tips of the laces untied to click across the tiled floor. "Did you find out who broke into my shop?"

Elroy shook his head. "This is a lot bigger than a B & E, Walker. You might want to call a lawyer or somebody to meet you down at the station."

"If this is routine, why would I need a lawyer?" He eyed the deputy suspiciously. "Just tell me what the questioning is about."

"I'll do that very thing, soon's we get to headquarters." The impatient edge to Elroy's voice was clearly audible.

Faith had heard enough. Her hands fisted at her waist, she glared at the deputy with fire in her eyes. "Now you listen to me, Elroy Pike," she huffed. "Law or not, you can't jerk Buddy Lee out of our home in the dark of night without telling him what the heck the accusations are. Who do you think you are?"

She was getting madder by the minute at the local law, and since she'd had more than a few skirmishes with them in her youth, she knew Elroy was an expert at blowing hot air. Not that he wasn't a good deputy, but he simply had a bad case of "I'm a Lawman. You're Not" when it came to doing things by the book. He didn't mean to be a pompous ass, he just was. And that was on his good days.

He held up his hands to shield against her verbal barrage. "Now, Faith, don't go getting on your high horse. There's no accusations. Just some questions."

"About what?" Buddy Lee all but shouted his frustration. "You got something to say, Elroy, you better go ahead and ask me now or forget it."

When he put his arm around her waist, Faith could feel the tension gathering along his muscles. She slid her arm around his back to present a united front. A sneaking suspicion said her daddy was behind whatever this was all about. Elroy gave them such a patronizing look right then, she wanted to aim a good kick at his shins. Or higher.

"We're staying right here until you explain what this is all about," Buddy Lee said.

"Oh, all right," Elroy snapped. "But I'm still gonna have to take you in. Dammit, I don't make the laws, I just uphold 'em. I don't know why you can't just cooperate. I *am* the deputy sheriff, you know." Shoving his hat back, he mopped perspiration from his brow with a pristine, white handkerchief.

A sauna couldn't be any steamier, Faith thought. Even at four o'clock in the morning, the air was saturated with the humidity of the Texas summer night, yet she stayed close to Buddy Lee's side. Something in Elroy's voice had fear tap-dancing up and down her spine. The dancing erupted into a full-fledged *Stomp* arrangement at Elroy's next words.

"It's like this. We just found Royce Webb's body in the ravine down by the old railroad crossing. Coroner's trying to determine cause of death." Elroy cleared his throat while his gaze zeroed in on Faith's bare legs, lingered a nano-second too long to suit her, then traveled up to her face. "Sorry I had to tell you like this, Faith. It would've been easier if Buddy Lee here had just let me take him in. I would've told him then. He's got to come with me, anyway."

Faith weaved unsteadily and was grateful for the support of her husband's strong arm. *Royce is dead? Dear God, do they suspect Buddy Lee?* She closed her eyes against the squeamish churning in her stomach, but popped them open again the minute she heard Elroy fire off a round of questions at Buddy Lee.

"Where were you tonight? Can you account for your time, say from around ten o'clock to just after midnight? Did anyone see you during that time?"

"I was working," came the clipped answer. The muscles in his jaw ticked, but he looked down at Faith with a reassuring smile. The warmth of his hand rubbing up and down her back soothed and comforted. Gave her hope and courage.

"Well, if you can prove it, Walker, then you've got nothing to worry about, have you?" Elroy said.

Faith stomped her foot and got right in the deputy's face. "Of course, he can prove it. Why would you doubt his word?"

Ignoring her, Elroy jerked his head toward the door. "We can finish this when we get to the station. Let's go."

She knew Buddy Lee couldn't possibly be capable of murder. Never. Besides, Elroy didn't know about Royce's assault. Or the reason for it. She wasn't about to let him find out, either.

Before Deputy Sheriff Elroy Pike could protest, she wagged her finger under his nose. "I'm going with you, Elroy. Wait right here while I change my clothes. And don't you dare take Buddy Lee away before I come back."

She gave her husband a quick kiss on the cheek and hurried to the bedroom.

The two men waited by the door, just as Faith had ordered.

For such an early hour, the police station in Granite City was buzzing with activity. Two hookers, decked out in identical black leather mini-skirts, their sequined tops tighter than tattoos, were arguing vehemently with the sergeant behind the desk while a belligerent, spike-haired, body-pierced, young boy about fifteen, wearing droopy, over-sized camo pants and shirt, waited for his angry parents to finish speaking with the arresting officer.

Faith knew exactly how the teen was feeling, the scene reminiscent of one or two of her own experiences. A particular one came to mind, when Buddy Lee had stood by her in this very same spot and boldly stated he was the one with the spray paint can, not her.

She cringed, remembering how she had kept silent and let him take the blame, along with the sentence of community service every Saturday for the next two months. Saturdays had been his days to work at the local gas station, so, of course, he'd lost his job. She hadn't realized then that the job was his only source of income. Yet he'd never said a word in his own defense. Not to the police or to her furious daddy, who told her to stay away from "white trash like that Walker boy."

Faith remembered pretending not to notice the grim set of Buddy Lee's mouth when he stormed past them, out of the police station. Remembered, too, that she hadn't seen much of him the rest of that summer. His daddy had been sent to prison, and to make up for the loss of his better paying job, Buddy Lee took up a night job stocking shelves at the supermarket. The graffiti on the water tower mysteriously disappeared overnight. Buddy Lee's doing, of course.

She felt small and unworthy of his friendship right now, yet her heart was so full of love and admiration for the boy he'd been and the man he'd become, she feared it would burst. She'd make it all up to this tender, caring man she'd fallen deeply in love with. Somehow.

Chapter Thirteen

Buddy Lee and Faith followed the deputy into a smaller office down the hall and took their seats in the only empty chairs in front of the desk.

An eerie sense of *déjà vu* swept over Buddy Lee. It had been a long time since he'd seen the inside of this place. Damn, it gave him the willies, being here with Faith again. He half expected her daddy to show up, spewing his familiar brand of criticisms like before.

Elroy hooked his hat on the hanger by the door and took a seat behind the cluttered desk. Buddy Lee thought the lawman looked a little too smug, but kept that opinion to himself. For now. Royce's death, no matter how it happened, couldn't be connected to *him*, since he'd been facing off with old man Morgan at the time.

He rubbed a hand over his face. Shoot, he couldn't tell the authorities where he'd been or why. That would mean explaining about his missing Mustang—which they were gonna find out anyway— and *that* would lead to questions about why he'd let Royce blackmail him in the first place. He sure as hell couldn't reveal Faith's secret. And where *was* his car, by the way? If it hadn't been found with Royce, he must have hidden it somewhere. Or maybe he'd already sold it.

His head started pounding with the mother of all headaches. No matter what he said, he was gonna wind up looking bad. How had his life landed in this swamp full of alligators in such a short time? The luck of being *Boyd's boy*, no doubt.

Elroy flipped through a stack of papers on his desk and pulled out one, picked up a ball-point pen and pointed it at Buddy Lee. "Now, let's get down to facts, Walker."

Faith jumped up before Buddy Lee could restrain her.

"You have the facts, Elroy." Her outburst was accompanied by a frenzy of arm-waving and fist-shaking. "He told you he was working. What part of that don't you understand?"

Buddy Lee grabbed her hand and pulled her back into the chair. "Hush, darlin'. Just hush." He turned his face away from the sheriff and lowered his voice so only she could hear him. "Don't say any more or you'll just make it worse. Please?"

She scowled at him like he was the enemy here and slumped back in her seat. He took that as a "Yes." At least, she wasn't yammering anymore. Sheese!

"Let's start with where you were at ten-thirty last night, and you tell me what you were doing right on up to about one o'clock this morning." Elroy got up and walked around to the front of the desk, hitched his hip on the edge and folded his arms across his chest. "Do you usually work that late? Was anyone there with you?"

Buddy Lee shook his head. "Nope." If Elroy wanted information, by damn, he was gonna have to figure it out himself. No way would he admit he was at Lionel's groveling for a favor. Putting Faith's secret on the line was not gonna happen, even if they held a gun to his head.

Elroy's smirk was enough to make him bite his tongue and clench his fists. Hellfire, he didn't want to start a brawl right here in the station house, but if Mr. Better-than-you-and-maybe-God Lawman didn't back off, that's exactly what would happen. And Pike could just quit ogling Faith, too. Damn lecher. He was married to her cousin, for cryin' out loud.

"That's interesting," Elroy said, stroking his chin and watching Faith scoot around in her chair while he kept on talking to Buddy Lee. "What exactly were you working on? That prized Mustang of yours?"

Oh, great, here it comes. Now Faith will find out I've lost the car. He kicked his brain into fast-forward, searched for a believable answer and wished for a more creative imagination.

"Well," he drawled, stalling for time while his thought process fired up its pistons, "matter of fact, I was just doin' some paper work. Not as interesting as working on the Mustang, but necessary."

Faith shot him a funny look. What the hell was that for?

"And just what time did you leave the garage? What did you do after you left? Go straight home?" Elroy raised an eyebrow in his direction, then pulled his mouth into a smarmy grin. "Of course, your wife would probably know when you came to bed, now wouldn't she?"

Buddy Lee wanted to pop him one right in his nasty mouth. He wanted Faith left out of this mess, but he could see Elroy was determined to drag them both through a whole pile before he was through. Was old man Morgan behind this, after all? Had someone really killed Royce? And where the hell *was* his Mustang?

Faith jumped up from her seat right then and jammed her fists on her hips. "I can tell you Buddy Lee was home in bed where he belonged, Elroy Pike. And what time he got there is no concern of yours, because I'm telling you he was with me all night. I'm his wife, and that's what I say." She shook a fist at him. "Now, go do your job and figure out what happened to Royce. Honestly, you watch too many crime shows on TV, Elroy. This is Buddy Lee. He's not a criminal and you know it."

Elroy slid off the edge of the desk to stand in front of them. "Yeah, I know who he is, Faith." He paused just long enough to let his implication sink in. "And we all know the apple doesn't fall far from the tree."

"Oh, stuff it, Elroy," Faith snapped. "You are so full of yourself."

"I can charge you with interfering with this investigation, *Cousin*, and that wouldn't help your husband here, at all. Better keep a lid on that sassy mouth of yours." The deputy cocked his head and stared right at her, his gaze homing in on her full lips. "It's gotten you in trouble more than once, if I remember."

"He's right, Faith," Buddy Lee interjected. "Just let him ask his questions, so we can go home."

He was secretly proud of the way she'd stood up for him, but that only made him feel like a first-class jackass for deceiving her. He didn't want her defending him like he was helpless or something, but he didn't want her to find out where he'd really been, either.

"Why don't you let Faith go on home, Elroy? I'll stay and answer your questions, just keep her out of this."

"I'm not going anywhere without you," Faith said stubbornly.

Good old Elroy hadn't bothered to close the door to his office and several curious officers on night duty strolled by, gawking as they passed. When one of them stopped and stuck his head in the door, Buddy Lee's heart landed in his sneakers.

Norm Atkins, Newcomb County's sheriff, favored everyone in the room with a raised eyebrow. "Trouble in here, Pike?"

Elroy pulled himself to attention. "No, sir, just routine questioning on the Webb homicide. Walker here was accounting for his whereabouts last night."

"And you've got good reason for this questioning?" Atkins' remarks were quiet and dead serious.

"Yessir," Elroy replied. "Everybody knows how Walker stole Webb's fiancée right from under his nose. Married her and ran off with her. Figured that was reason enough to make him a suspect. They could've argued, fought over Faith. Then Webb turns up murdered. Suspicious, sir."

"Far as I know, Pike, marriage isn't a crime. And cause of death in the Webb case hasn't been determined yet, so don't label it a homicide 'til you have all the facts. Stick to protocol, or you'll be in trouble, too." Atkins nodded to Faith, shot Buddy Lee a curious look, then left the room.

"See, Elroy, even your boss thinks you're jumping to conclusions." Faith edged closer to Buddy Lee and tucked her hand in his. "I hope you find the person responsible for Royce's death, if that's what really happened. But Buddy Lee and I don't know anything about it. So let us go home."

"She's right, Elroy. We've answered all your questions. You don't have any reason to keep us here." Jeez, he sure hoped that was true. If Elroy ever got ahold of the fact he'd been over at Lionel's last night—and why—no telling what would hit the fan then. He needed to get Faith home before that happened.

With his hand on the small of her back, he guided her toward the door. If Elroy wanted to, he could detain him, but Faith was goin' home, no matter what.

The deputy nodded, but the dour expression on his face told Buddy Lee the lawman was clearly p.o.'d at the way things were turning out. Well, hoo-ha. He wasn't exactly shoutin' *hallelujah*, either.

It was just after five in the morning when the two finally followed a very angry Elroy outside to the patrol car. Newcomb County's finest returned the couple home in complete silence.

Faith didn't wait long before she dropped her bombshell. One hand on her hip, a wooden spoon in the other, she stopped in the middle of what she was doing at the kitchen stove and turned around, sparks of disapproval flickering in her eyes.

"What will you do without the car, Buddy Lee?"

He lowered his gaze, suddenly absorbed in a hangnail on his clenched hand. If she'd planned on landing a sucker-punch, she sure hit her mark. An automatic reflex tightened his gut, and he glanced up from where he sat at the kitchen table just in time to see the mulishly stubborn set to her mouth.

Buddy Lee braced himself. *Oh, man, here it comes.* The one question he'd hoped to avoid as long as possible. He didn't know exactly how he was going to explain it to her, but he figured he'd better put some serious thought to the matter real quick. Or maybe he should try distracting her. Yeah, he could do that. Much easier than answering her question.

"Well?" She waggled the wooden spoon she'd been using on the egg mixture at him. Her eyebrows shot up in little peaks and her mouth pulled into a thin line. "You might as well come clean because I am so mad at you right now, I can't think straight. How could you give away something as valuable as that Mustang? To Royce, for heaven's sake! What were you thinking?"

She tossed the spoon on the countertop and waved her hands in agitation. "And furthermore, I know you intended to sell it, so don't tell me you didn't need it. Good grief, Buddy Lee, do you know you just gave away a fortune? That was your only chance to pay off the bank and keep from losing the business you've worked so hard to build. Do you know what that...?"

Slapping his hand on the tabletop, he knocked over his chair in the process of jumping to his feet. "I know what the hell I did, Faith. And why. So, just let me worry about it." He wasn't gonna have her fretting over his damn financial screw-up. "I took care of a problem, that's all."

"And Royce was the problem, wasn't he?" Her voice wavered, but her rigid stance told him she wasn't giving an inch. Her mama should've named her Stubborn.

Shoot, she hadn't said two words all the way home from the police station, and that in itself was enough to make him nervous as all get out. 'Cause Faith not talking was downright scary. Especially when she was mad. Now she couldn't hush up.

When he'd asked if she felt okay, she'd just nodded and said she was planning. Boy, did that ever set his nerves to jangling. *Faith* and *planning* was a combination that had gotten him bogged down in the alligator swamp more than once.

Then she'd started scrambling eggs and making toast as soon as they got home, saying she was hungry and too upset to go back to bed. Hell, he'd figured climbing back in bed would be a real fine solution for solving their mutual frustration. He sure wasn't hungry for eggs. But her question about his missing Mustang came right out of the blue. Blindsided him. How had she found out the car was gone? She couldn't have gone to the shop.

He heaved a sigh deep enough to make him shudder. Right now, his life was about as stable as a runaway rollercoaster.

"I didn't kill him, if that's what you're asking." He took a step toward her. "Look at me, Faith. Do you honestly believe I could do that?"

She shook her head and sighed. "I don't know what to think, anymore. I never dreamed any of this craziness would happen. Never believed I'd be pregnant with Royce's child."

Her eyes grew bright with tears and her anger softened to bewilderment. "I never thought I'd be married to you, either, Buddy Lee."

"Life kinda surprised both of us, darlin'." His heart was crowding his throat, making his voice crack in mid-sentence. "You knew I didn't have much when you asked me to marry you, but I promised to take care of you the best way I could. Did you believe me? 'Cause if you didn't, then why in hell did you let me love you?" *Well, damn, he hadn't meant to say that.*

When she gasped out a shocked sob, he reckoned if dumb was dirt, he'd cover about an acre.

Ever since that very first time when they'd made love, he couldn't seem to get enough of her, but for him, there was more to it than the physical part. He needed her to believe in him, to trust him again. He wanted her to need him for more than just a way out of her problem.

He sauntered over to his flea-market special boom-box on the counter, latched on to the first tape in a nearby stack, and shoved it into the slot. Music was a good way to start his 'distracting' strategy.

Whoa! The volume must've been cranked up to bust-an-eardrum level, 'cause Willie and Julio started belting out something about all the girls they'd loved before, and Faith's eyes widened in astonishment.

He hit the Eject button so fast the tape jetted across the room like a missile. He didn't bother to retrieve it, just left it on the floor where it landed and hurried to pick out a more appropriate, mood-setting one. He hoped.

Sure enough, as the soft, mellow strain of a Mickey Gilley ballad filled the tiny room with a pure Country love song, he saw Faith's body slowly sway back and forth with the bluesy rhythm, and he grinned all the way to his toes. Bingo!

His hands found her waist, pulled her close. He drew a deep breath and let her very essence seep into his soul. God, she smelled so good, fit so perfectly nestled up against him. His body responded instantly to her nearness. He was in Heaven, if only for a little while.

"Dance with me," he murmured against her cheek, and looped her arms around his neck.

At first, she stiffened in his embrace, but he kept right on moving with the only dance he knew how to do, until he felt her melt against him. Ahhh! If there was one thing he knew he did well, it was this. *Give me a smooth, slow dance any day.* He didn't know any of those fancy, city-slicker steps, but he was pretty sure swaying together like this had formal, ballroom footwork beat all to heck and back.

Now, with Faith pressed tight against him, their bodies moving as one while Mickey G. crooned about lonely nights and forgettin' about tomorrow, Buddy Lee figured this *distracting* thing was working out pretty good. It sure had his thoughts moving right along to other things besides cops and cars and bein' flat broke. And he had a sneakin' suspicion Faith was a little distracted, too.

"Mmmmm, uh, Faith...?" he said, real cautious like, thinking maybe he was on the right track here, but not wanting to give the impression sex was the only thing he ever thought about.

She didn't say anything and that worried him some, because she hadn't spoken since he'd begun to dance with her—just kept following his lead, doing that swayin' thing with her hips that was slowly driving him crazy. Jeez! She had to be feeling the same way he was. Why else would she be giving him this come-on with her body, as well as her eyes?

He hoped she'd forgotten her question about the car by now. He was doin' his best to make sure she did. He'd pretty much forgotten it himself, as other, more pressing things, occupied his mind. Time enough later for that particular show and tell. Especially with the possibility of a homicide still hanging over them like a black cloud of doom.

Her response was to nuzzle her head into the hollow of his shoulder while her fingers wandered up and down the back of his neck. Her summer-sweet fragrance shot straight to his brain. He stumbled, missed a step, and fought back the dangerous combination of light-headedness and tight jeans that was ganging up on him.

"Sweet mercy," he breathed and danced her down the hallway toward the bedroom. He prayed the music never stopped.

Darn him, Faith fumed silently, as she followed the suggestive rhythm of Buddy Lee's low-down-and-dirty glide and slide. She'd always been a pushover for emotional Country love songs. One more mark in his favor.

When he had folded her in his arms and two-stepped her around the kitchen floor, her first reaction had been to stomp on his toes, but her body took on a mind of its own, moving instinctively to the sensuous beat of Mickey Gilley's torchy ballad and the invitation of Buddy Lee's hard body. She didn't stand a chance against that kind of seduction, thank you very much, Mr. G. and Mr. W.

Not that she really objected. If she were honest—and she was trying to improve on that—she truly enjoyed it. There was something about the universal, unspoken language of slow-dancing that left no doubt as to what was being said. The silent conversing of bodies, the secret words expressed with a touch, a caress, or just a long, slow look—all these spoke loud and clear of heated desires and urgent needs. No *Webster's Tenth* needed here. Faith's own needs were clearly defined by now, and Buddy Lee's were more than obvious.

Her mind still hung on to a few sensible thoughts, though. One being that this seductive dancing was absurd when she was supposed to be finding out why he gave the car to Royce in the first place, and why Royce was dead. That was the important issue. Had Royce actually been murdered? Her blood chilled at that possibility. Buddy Lee was the most likely suspect in the crime, thanks to Elroy's suspicious mind.

He did have a motive, she supposed. Without his valuable Mustang, there'd be no money to pay off his loan. And even if he proved his innocence in Royce's death, he was bound to lose his shop and his livelihood. Wouldn't that make Daddy overjoyed? A chance to point out another of his daughter's endless mistakes. She wondered if he kept a list of the ones she'd made through the years.

That possibility should have worried her, but right now, her husband was seducing her with a two-step. How absurd was that? Was it just the hormonal change taking place in her body? Her pregnancy? Or was it the feel of his *body language* rubbing against her as they danced toward the bedroom?

She floated with him as they tumbled onto the bed, the serious stuff just getting started.

In about an hour or so, I'll ask him about the car again, Faith promised herself. Honest. Right after we have this intimate body-language *conversation*.

Afterwards, Faith lay quietly next to him, listening to his steady breathing. There was something beautiful about the afterglow of Buddy Lee's lovemaking. Something special she'd never felt before. Did he feel as lucky as she did? They'd married because of her monumental mistake, but they'd found something she hadn't expected. Could it be love? Once the baby arrived, would Buddy Lee be able to see beyond the child's paternity? Was it fair to even ask that of him? Could they be a real family, or would he want to leave then? So many questions, so many doubts and fears for the future.

She eased up on one elbow and gazed down at her husband. He looked so peaceful. She wondered how he could sleep with all the turmoil in their life right now. Her own mind buzzed with so many fractured thoughts, she had trouble separating them as they flew around in her brain. Too many unanswered questions: Royce's death, the car, the loan due tomorrow. Tomorrow? Oh no! Tomorrow was already here!

Spurred by the sudden realization that time was running out, she slipped out of bed, grabbed some clean clothes and headed for the shower, praying the ancient water pipes wouldn't rattle too loudly. An idea that had been brewing in her mind since yesterday began to take shape.

By the time she'd eaten a raisin bagel and finished her orange juice, the sun had already heated the morning air to a muggy eighty-two degrees. As she reflected on her effort to get Buddy Lee to talk about his plight, she dumped the earlier attempt at eggs into the trash along with two rock-hard pieces of cold toast, then rinsed her juice glass.

No, *their* plight, she amended. She was in this as deep, or deeper, than he was. If it wasn't for her stupid recklessness, there'd be no plight to deal with.

On her way to the refrigerator with the carton of juice, she punched Play on the tape player and turned the volume down low. Mickey Gilley's seductive voice sang to her this time about true love ways. Her heart stumbled, remembering. Leave it to Buddy Lee to use honky-tonk blues music and sweet-talking lyrics to tell her what he couldn't say out loud.

She hadn't known he was such a smooth dancer. No wonder the girls in school had always tried to convince him to show up at the school dances. He never asked them out, though. She should have wondered about that at the time, but she'd been too busy planning her next rebellion against her daddy to pay attention. Too busy looking for love in all the wrong places.

Back then, Buddy Lee had been a pal as well as her protector. And she'd been a foolish, mixed-up young girl who didn't know a good thing when it stood right in front of her. She'd been so blind. How lucky she'd finally gotten a chance to discover the important things in life. To discover the loving side of Buddy Lee Walker. Even if she didn't deserve it.

She peeked in the bedroom. Thank goodness, she could slip away before he woke up. She didn't want him trying to protect her from her daddy's wrath that would surely come down on her head. This was something she had to do on her own. For Buddy Lee, for herself, and for the future she hoped they would share.

She dashed off a quick note saying she was going to check on her mama. She hoped he believed her.

If she hurried, she could catch her daddy before he left for the bank. If she was lucky, her mama would still be in bed. She didn't think she could deal with more than one problem at a time.

Chapter Fourteen

Buddy Lee came awake with a startled jerk, momentarily forgetting where he was and wondering if he'd already been tried and found guilty. There'd been a trial and a jury in his dreams, one that convicted him—not for committing a crime—but for being *Boyd's boy.*

Cold sweat slicked his bare skin. He reached for Faith, for reassurance that he was really home and not behind bars. Panic whopped him when nothing but empty space met his seeking hand. He rolled over, ready to believe the worst. Then a replay of the early morning session at the police station kicked in, and he remembered how Faith had jumped to his defense.

How about the way she went after ol' Elroy? Man, she was all over that cousin of hers like ugly on an ape, shaking her fist at him and giving him what for. She'd been a regular spitfire, proclaiming her husband's innocence loud and clear to anyone within shouting distance. And he *was* innocent, dammit.

He wouldn't deny that he despised Royce Webb. The world would be better off without scum like his wife's ex-fiancé. And yeah, he'd tried to pound him to a pulp when he'd threatened Faith's safety. If the jerk hadn't run off, leaving him to make tracks to get Faith to a doctor, no telling how much damage he'd have done to him. But murder? No way. One Walker behind bars was more than enough.

Fresh from a quick shower, he made his way to the kitchen in search of his wife and, hopefully, a good-morning kiss. All he found was coffee and another damned note on the counter. *Aw, come on, Faith.* Was this some kind of weird game of hers, leaving a note then disappearing while he was asleep? If she intended to torment him, she was succeeding big time.

He snatched up the piece of paper, read the few words and tossed it on the table. At least this time she'd told him where she was going. He couldn't very well blame her for wanting to see her mama, so he tried to shove aside his disappointment at not having her, all sleepy-eyed and warm, to wake up with.

He'd been looking forward to spending some quality time with her this morning before he went to work. Precious time he felt they needed in order to explore their feelings, define their hopes and dreams, and decide whether or not their future together even had a snowball's chance.

Oh, he knew he could probably find a job at halfway decent wages. He was a damned good mechanic, and as long as trucks and cars kept rolling off the assembly lines, there'd be a need for someone to repair them.

But his hope of achieving his dream—that burning need to be more than just *Boyd's boy*—had disappeared when he gave up his treasured Mustang. Without it, there was nothing left. The years of sacrifice and hard work meant zip now. He had a wife to support. And a baby on the way that wasn't his. Just thinking about *that* hatched a whole slew of doubts about his sanity. Even though he'd promised to be the daddy, he wondered if he could honestly keep a pledge like that. One that challenged him to be the kind of man worthy of being called "Daddy." Or would he always look at the child and see Royce? Was he strong enough to endure the torment of living with Faith, knowing another man had given her a child?

And there was always the possibility that she intended to end their marriage after the baby was born. They'd never seriously discussed any plans beyond the birth. Shoot, he'd just taken it for granted that he'd be around, a part of their future. Maybe that had been wishful thinking on his part.

He sat drinking his coffee and wallowing in self-pity until the phone rang.

"Yeah?" he snapped into the mouthpiece.

"Walker, you need to get over to the sheriff's office right away," Elroy Pike told him.

"Wanna explain why?" His mood was just resentful enough to be nasty, even if it did add another alligator to the swamp. Hell, one more wouldn't make any difference now.

"Let's just say it's in your best interest."

Jeez. He had a sudden urge to tell Elroy where he could shove his superior attitude. He snapped his mouth shut instead because, after all, the sheriff was the law and Buddy Lee was tiptoeing mighty close to the lock-up door.

So he swallowed his angry retort. "I'll be there in thirty minutes, Elroy." He glanced at the kitchen clock. "And tell your boys to lay off their radar when they see my truck."

He plunked the receiver down before Newcomb County's finest had a chance to spout a response. Draining his coffee cup in one gulp, he grabbed an apple from the fridge and headed out the door. Helluva way to start the day.

"**H**ello, Daddy." Faith stood in the doorway to the familiar dining room of her parents' home. Surprised to find the front door unlocked, she'd quietly let herself in without knocking. Avoiding giving her daddy advance notice of her arrival was definitely in her favor.

Lionel Morgan glanced away from reading the morning business news, and a glower darkened his face the instant he recognized his caller.

"You have no reason to be here. See yourself out." He snapped the newspaper and returned his full attention to it.

Faith studied her father's profile, visible from where she stood. He seemed to have grown older since she'd last seen him just a few days before. His face was lined and slightly puffy, with a weariness she'd never noticed clouding his eyes. But his tongue had lost none of its razor-like sharpness.

He'd always been able to cut her down with a look or a single word, constantly reminding her that she was a Morgan with a reputation in the community to uphold. *Like she could ever forget.*

She quickly erected her own personal invisible shield against the hurtful tirade she knew would come, and strode into the room. "I have *every* reason to be here."

Lionel laid the paper down on the table, and pushing his chair back, started to rise.

Faith caught him by the arm. "No, Daddy, don't try to ignore me this time. Sit down. There's something important I want you to hear, so I'll talk and you'll listen."

Obviously stunned by her tenacity, Lionel sat back down. Then his gray eyes narrowed and his mouth thinned. Once again he was the inflexible parent of her youth.

Faith quickly took a seat opposite him at the table, and remembering what was at stake, drew courage from somewhere deep inside and plunged into her speech before she lost her nerve.

"I found out about your underhanded trick to call in Buddy Lee's note—" Her father started to protest, but she charged on. "Did you stop to think about everyone your spitefulness might hurt? Of course not. As usual, it's always about the money." She leaned toward him. "Well, you know what? Money is the only company you're going to have in your old age, because I won't be here and neither will your first grandchild."

Regret squeezed her heart. She was bidding a final good-bye to a parent who refused to let love enrich his life.

She'd always felt invisible around her daddy. At first she'd looked to her mama for support, but that never happened. Beryl Morgan was so intimidated by her husband that she never crossed him, rarely disputed his word. To say she was submissive would be the understatement of the year. So with sadness, Faith acknowledged the very real possibility that her mama would stand by him.

Sorry for the few family ties being cut, she hugged her arms to her chest and eyed her father sitting silently, jaw set in a stubborn line. "You'll never know the joy of bouncing that baby on your knee or having tiny arms hug your neck.

Never cuddle a little one close to your heart or sing sweet lullabies. You missed that happiness with your own child."

She struggled to keep her voice level as she added, "All I ever wanted was for you to love me for myself, not as a reflection of the Morgan money. My child will be rich with love instead of cold cash. I pity you, Daddy. I really do."

Gulping air to steady herself, she saw his expression change and felt a trace of satisfaction. It looked as if he was regarding her for the first time as an individual with valid opinions and the right to be respected for them.

But he shattered that illusion quickly.

Lionel's face reddened. His breathing grew harsh, his eyes flashed. "Ungrateful! You've always been ungrateful for all the privileges the name Morgan afforded you. Now you come in here and accuse me of underhandedness? You choose the white trash you're sleeping with over your family?" He stabbed the newspaper with his finger. "According to this, your husband is a suspect in Royce Webb's murder. Hhmmph! Like father, like son."

"Like father, like son"...No, Daddy, like father like daughter.

By the time she was twelve, Faith had concluded that her parents were united against her. Thus, the rebellion of her teen years had become her prime ambition. She'd worked hard at it, too. Ask anyone in town.

Then Buddy Lee began to act as a buffer between her wild escapades and her irate parent, making her acts of defiance that much easier. As her friend, he could always be counted on to pick up after her and occasionally take the blame to save her skin. And she'd been selfish enough to let him, disregarding any hurt or humiliation he might have suffered on her account.

Had she subconsciously thought that because of his name, he had no feelings? The suspicion that her actions back then made her no better than her father sickened her.

"Buddy Lee didn't kill Royce." She didn't want to cry. But right then, guilty tears burned behind her eyes, ready to spill at the slightest provocation.

How could she have known this would hurt so much? She swallowed back the tears. Her heart felt poked full of holes, and all the love she'd saved up to share with her parents was leaking out. But she couldn't talk rationally while blubbering through a waterfall, so she laced her fingers together in her lap, gripped them tight, and talked faster.

"What if I told you the baby isn't Buddy Lee's? That the father is Royce, who betrayed everyone's trust. A man who only cared about money. Like you, Daddy."

"What do you mean?" Lionel barked. "Of course, the kid is a Walker. You said so, yourself. You and Boyd Walker's boy ran off and got married and humiliated us all. Shamed the Morgan name."

Lionel's voice boomed across the room like a cannon's echo, but Faith refused to be browbeaten any longer. "No I didn't. What *you're* doing is shameful. You never tried to understand. Never cared enough to be there when I needed you. Now you're getting revenge by punishing Buddy Lee for something he had nothing to do with. Nothing, you hear? You're destroying his business when you should be helping him build it for your grandchild's security. A child that has Morgan blood. Your blood."

She shuddered and took a deep breath. "Buddy Lee is a bigger man than you'll ever be, because he didn't condemn me or turn his back on me when I needed help. Because he's decent and willing to marry me so an innocent child that's not even his could have a father—and a name. Because," her voice broke, snagged on a sob, "because my baby's unscrupulous father is dead, and I don't even care. All the money in your bank won't buy what really matters. Love and respect."

The tears came now in torrents. She buried her head in her hands and let them flow unchecked. She had more to explain, much more to reveal, but right now she needed the cleansing release that crying brought to her anguished heart.

A hand pressed lightly on her shoulder, so faint she barely felt it. A gentle hand that had been too long absent in giving solace, but Faith's bruised heart recognized the touch immediately.

"Mama?"

Beryl Morgan tenderly stroked her daughter's cheek. "I'm here, Faith, where I should've been a long time ago. I heard everything. I'm so sorry. Can you forgive me?" Then she turned to her husband, one comforting hand still on Faith's shoulder.

"She's right, you know, Lionel." Despite the soft tone, Beryl's words packed a punch. "We're both guilty of dereliction of duty as parents. You believed money and prestige substituted for love. You were wrong. By letting you control our lives, I thought I was being a dutiful wife and loving mother." She shook her head, eyes filled with sadness. "Both terrible mistakes. Because of our warped sense of duty, our misplaced pride, we're about to lose the most precious gift God ever gave us—our child. Think about it, Lionel. I don't want to lose a grandchild, too."

Beryl left Faith's side, and with head high and clear determination strode over to stand beside her husband's chair. There was no mistaking the new mantle of strength she had taken.

Faith's heart swelled with love for this fragile woman who, after all these years, had finally found the courage to demand the respect she deserved.

"If you don't tell your son-in-law, and yes, I mean Buddy Lee Walker, that you'll extend his loan without interest *and* go to the sheriff to confirm his air-tight alibi for the night of

Royce's death, then I'll be moving out, too." She paused and looked Lionel straight in the eye. "And don't think I'll hesitate to go to Elroy if you decide not to. Buddy Lee was here that night, and I'll sign a statement to the effect. I don't want to give up a chance to be a part of our daughter's and our grandchild's life, and if I have to do it without you, so be it.

I've waited too long to have real love in my life."

Lionel squirmed in his seat. "Blast it, Beryl," his fist hit the table, "haven't I given you everything you asked for? You've got the biggest house in town, expensive clothes, luxury car. What more do you need?" He slumped back in his chair, clearly puzzled by his wife's demands.

"You truly don't know, do you, Lionel?" Beryl placed both hands on the table and leaned toward him. "Maybe if you think seriously about what your own life has become, you'll understand and do the right thing. Is losing your family worth the money you consider so important? Do you want to grow old all alone?" Taking a deep breath that shuddered clear through her, the newly-confident Beryl Morgan squared her frail shoulders. "I don't intend to."

Faith rushed forward and flung her arms around her mama in a long overdue hug that had them both smiling through their tears. "I love you, Mama. So much."

Beryl hugged her back. "I love you, too, child. And I suspect you love Buddy Lee, as well."

"I do," came Faith's adamant reply as mother and daughter stood arm-in-arm. "But I'm not sure he feels the same way. Helping me has cost him everything he's worked for, and unless a miracle happens, he'll lose his business. He must regret ever seeing me again, since I've been nothing but trouble for him for as long as I can remember."

Beryl moved from her daughter's side and stood across the room to gaze out of the window. After a long pause, she turned her attention from the perfectly groomed gardens outside to the daughter who needed her now more than ever.

"Something tells me Buddy Lee wouldn't make such a sacrifice if he didn't care a great deal about you, sweetheart. That he offered to give your child his name says a great deal about his sincerity. Obviously, you mean more to him than money."

"Ha!" Lionel scoffed. "He's smart enough to know he needs the Morgan money to keep from losing that business of his."

"That's where you're wrong, Lionel. Buddy Lee loves Faith."

The pointed look her mama sent her daddy right then was filled with newfound feminine courage, and Faith silently applauded.

"Do you really think so?" She wanted to believe her mama more than anything, but her own usual self-confidence was in danger of slipping.

"Of course, dear. I would consider myself lucky to have that kind of love. A love worth fighting for."

Lionel *harrumphed* loudly a time or two until the women stopped talking and turned their attention to him. "You said there was more to your story," he muttered. "I suppose I can spare the time to listen."

His attempt to regain control of the situation didn't surprise Faith. She never expected her daddy's unbending ways to change overnight, but with her mama offering loving support, maybe revealing the ugly truth about Royce wouldn't be too difficult.

Might as well get it over with, she thought, and pulled out a chair for her mother.

"Sit down, Mama. Daddy, don't interrupt until I'm through talking, you hear?"

Chapter Fifteen

Buddy Lee whipped into the parking lot of the Newcomb County courthouse, parked, and strode into the red brick building with two minutes to spare. Elroy had made good on his request to keep the highway boys looking the other way.

The deputy was standing outside his office door, apparently waiting for him. Behind the open door, Buddy Lee caught a brief glimpse of...that couldn't be Morgan in there, could it?

Before he could get a better look, Elroy yanked the door shut.

"Walker," he addressed him with a nod, "before we go in, I've got something to say."

"Yeah?" He figured Elroy was probably fixin' to say Faith's old man had brought another trumped-up charge against him to add to his growing collection. Why else would the banker be in there? Sure, the note was due today, but the bank didn't close for a few hours. Four o'clock was the end of the bank's business day and, ironically, the end of his entire business. Sheese! The damned alligators were takin' over the swamp.

"Lionel Morgan's in there," Elroy jerked his thumb toward his office. "Says he can verify your whereabouts last night.   Why didn't you tell me that? You could've saved us all a lot of time in this investigation. And paperwork."

Buddy Lee couldn't have been more surprised if one of those alligators had asked him to dance. *What is going on?* He craned his neck and tried to look around Elroy's brown-uniformed shape to get a glimpse of Faith's daddy. If word got around that he'd gone to Lionel—and why—Faith's secret was bound to be exposed. Didn't make any sense.

"Did Morgan say why he was gonna do that?" Better be careful not to say more than necessary, just in case his father-in-law had some wild idea to implicate him in something besides Royce's death. He'd learned early on to keep his mouth shut and watch his back.

"Guess you'll have to ask him yourself," Elroy stated. "But I apologize for jumping to conclusions. Should've checked my facts more carefully." The deputy's face reddened and he stuck out his hand.

The gesture of apology took Buddy Lee by surprise, but he wasn't so dumb as to ignore it. The men shook hands, then Elroy turned and opened the door.

The electrical currents zinging through the office could have powered to the whole town. Beside Elroy's desk, Lionel

Morgan sat in a straight-back chair, body rigid as cast-iron. Seated next to him, Beryl Morgan looked amazingly calm and confident. Not a bit like the woman Buddy Lee had known most of his life. No longer a shadowy extension of her husband, she exuded an air of self-assurance that puzzled him and set him to wondering.

Faith stood beside her mother's chair, looking happy as a cat with one paw in a fishbowl. She flashed him a mega-watt smile and his heart flip-flopped. He had an eerie feeling everyone here knew something he didn't. And that wasn't a comfortable feeling, at all. Neither was his sneaking suspicion that Faith had been *planning* again.

And what was Beryl grinning about? She never *grinned*, for cryin' out loud. Hardly ever smiled, come to think of it. Had somebody spiked the water fountain?

Faith spoke first. "Hey, Buddy Lee."

At first, he couldn't get his damned tongue unstuck from the roof of his mouth. Then after a couple false starts, his tongue finally cooperated. "Hey, Faith. Wanna tell me what's going on?"

"Sure, but why don't you ask Daddy? He's got all the facts."

Noooo, Buddy Lee protested silently. Not all of 'em, he hoped. "Your daddy?" He needed to sit down before his legs buckled under him.

He fell into the nearest chair as Elroy fiddled with a palm-sized tape recorder. "Y'all don't mind if I tape this, do you? For the record, you know. It's required."

"If that's the rule, then go ahead, Deputy Pike," Beryl said softly.

Her formal use of Elroy's title made the lawman perk right up, and Lionel glower. He placed the machine on his desk, facing them, then pushed "record," and the whirr of the tape broke the silence that followed Beryl's words.

Just then, Faith sent Buddy Lee such a sweet smile he nearly melted on the spot. A shiver raced up his spine, and he had to order himself to get his act together. How was he gonna find out anything if he couldn't keep his mind on what mattered?

He looked at Elroy for help, got ignored, and turned to Lionel. What else could he do?

"Looks like you're the one's got something to tell *me*, so I guess you might as well start."

Faith's daddy acted like he had a helluva pain somewhere. He kept squirming in his chair, scowling, clearing his throat, and squirming some more.

Get to the damned point, he wanted to yell, but didn't. He'd made up his mind not to let Lionel yank his chain any more. Waiting was one thing he was good at. Slow-dancing was the other, but there wasn't any music playing here, so he just tipped his chair back on its hind legs and acted like he had more time than money. *Well, hoo-ha, don't I just?*

"Daddy." Faith had a way of giving a single word a multitude of meanings. Buddy Lee figured Lionel was smart enough to know when the meanings were serious.

"All right, all right," Morgan groused. "Walker, I'm gave the deputy here an alibi for you, since there doesn't seem to be any other way to save your hide. But only because Faith's got her mind set on you and her mama's threatening to leave me."

"Faith *what*?" He looked at her in disbelief. What had she done?

"And another thing," Lionel went on, ignoring Buddy Lee's slack jaw. "I've decided to forgive your note. I know Royce was blackmailing you and why. Faith told us everything." His face darkened. "Even about the abuse. I can't hold it against you for trying to keep my daughter's reputation from being smeared. Guess you'd know all about that sort of thing, seeing as how you're Boyd's...."

"Lionel," his wife cautioned in a soft, no-mistaking-what-she-meant tone.

"Daddy," his daughter warned in a voice as soft as her mama's, but much more threatening.

Lionel frowned, gave a deep sigh of resignation. "What I meant to say was, well, that was a decent thing you did, taking on a kid...er, my grandchild, to raise. The boy will be a Morgan, of course, so I'll expect him to be raised right."

Faith shook her head. "And if we have a girl, she'll be a Morgan, too, but the last name will always be Walker, Daddy. Remember that and be happy for us. Oh, and how we raise the child will be for Buddy Lee and me to decide."

Faith gazed lovingly at her husband, sea-green eyes gleaming with all sorts of temptations and promises. "That is, if Buddy Lee still agrees."

His insides knotted. If *I agree?* He wondered if it'd be impolite to holler "Hallelujah!" Good sense told him not.

"That thing still on?" he asked, pointing to the recorder.

"Yeah, why?" Elroy replied.

"Just want to make sure what I say gets put on that tape."

He paused a minute to sort out his words...decide what he wanted to say. He couldn't afford to mess up this time.

"As far as marrying Faith goes, well, for the record, I didn't do it just to be nice. And I damn sure didn't do it for Morgan money." He paused, took a deep breath and plunged ahead. "I did it because I love her. Always have."

He could feel her eyes boring right into him, but he couldn't bring himself to meet her gaze. Not yet. He needed to keep his head clear to finish what he had to say. Looking at her only made him want to take her in his arms and love her like crazy until her troubles went away. Since he'd already tried that and only created more grief, he knew better than to let himself be tempted again. He kept staring at the floor.

"I'll take care of her and her baby for as long as she needs me. I'm not sayin' I'll know how to love the child, but because Faith is the mama and I love her, I'll do my best to be the kind of father I think a kid oughta have. And the kind of husband I think Faith deserves, if she'll have me."

Slowly, he raised his head. Now he could look at her. He'd said what he'd been feeling all along. He'd work on learning to love their baby and he'd be a good father. That much he could promise. And if Faith wanted him in spite of that...well, here he was, faults and all.

She started to speak, but he held up his hand, then turned to Lionel. "One more thing. About the bank note that's due today. I don't accept charity from anyone, Mr. Morgan. Ever. So don't go forgiving my mortgage just so you can act like a do-gooder. All I need is an extension. This Walker pays his debts. And by the way, how come you decided to vouch for my whereabouts last night? I know you didn't have to."

"Like hell I didn't." Lionel came up off his chair. "Do you know my own wife threatened to leave me if I didn't tell Elroy where you were? And Faith called me a selfish old man because I wouldn't acknowledge the child she carries as my grandchild." He raked shaky fingers through his silver hair. "I've given her everything money can buy. How can that be selfish?"

"Maybe money couldn't buy what she wanted," Buddy Lee said. "Far as I know, love isn't for sale."

Lionel studied him a minute then sat down, hands gripping the arms of the chair. "Have you any idea how terrifying these two women can be when they decide to gang up on you?"

Buddy Lee had a pretty good notion, but figured that wasn't ever gonna be a problem for him. He was relieved to be cleared of any suspicion surrounding Royce's death, but wasn't sure he liked having Faith and her mama force Lionel's hand. Did that mean he'd be behind bars if Faith hadn't confronted her folks with her devastating secret? That he still had no credibility of his own? Hell, he was supposed to be taking care of her, not the other way around.

Elroy shut off the tape recorder. Faith nodded her head slightly. With an answering nod, he pulled a folder from his desk drawer, and tossed it on top. "Here's something else you might find interesting. Found these in your car."

"My car?" Buddy Lee hollered, not even worrying about good manners.

"Yep, the Mustang. And you don't need to yell, Walker," Elroy added. "I can hear just fine. The car's at Faith's new house. Guess ol' Webb stashed it there. The glove compartment was stuffed full of these." He shoved the folder across the desk toward Buddy Lee. "I.O.U.'s, every one. He was so deep in debt I guess he tried to sell your car to save his skin. Seems he had a double deal going with some thug connected to a Louisiana casino racketeer, but the whole thing backfired on him. Royce had pieces of his murderer's flesh under his fingernails where he'd tried to fight him off, poor bastard. Samples matched up with one of Boots Ogden's thugs over in Lake Charles. Forensic report showed he squeezed the life right outta Webb. Suspect's being held down there until his extradition. Big son-of-a-gun, too." Elroy slipped the papers back in the folder.

Lionel remained silent while the deputy recounted the details of his employee's death, but as soon as Elroy finished, the banker rose from his chair, face flushed with anger.

"And to think that crook had been lying to me all this time. I trusted him with my bank's finances." He slammed his fist down on Elroy's desk. "Come on, Beryl. I have to call my attorney and the bank auditor. By God, if that S.O.B. stole any funds from the bank, I'll...."

Elroy put a restraining hand on Lionel's arm. "The sheriff will be in touch, Lionel. Embezzlement's a serious charge, even if the suspect is dead, so go ahead and notify your auditor. We'll take care of getting in touch with the other authorities."

"You can be sure I will." Lionel shrugged off Pike's hand. "If I ever get out of here." Still angry and impatient he shuffled from one foot to the other, but his wife remained seated.

Elroy turned his attention back to Buddy Lee, not even trying to hide a smirk. "By the way, Walker, your Mustang's been impounded as evidence. Shame you signed the title over. When the investigation's finished it'll be auctioned off, and the judge will decide where the money will go."

Buddy Lee's head was spinning again. That happened a lot lately—every time he'd tried to figure things out. "So, this whole thing is over?" Even though he'd lost his car, this still seemed too simple. He looked over at Faith. She smiled at him like she'd planned the whole thing. That wouldn't surprise him.

Elroy nodded. "Far as you're concerned, yep. Just don't leave town for a few days, in case we have more questions. Y'all can all go home now."

"About time," Lionel grumbled and headed for the door. He stopped midway, turned back, hesitating before he held out a trembling hand. "Beryl, will you come home with me? Please?"

Beryl Morgan drew a deep breath, smiled at her husband, then patted Faith's arm. "You know where to find me, dear, if you need me."

Faith kissed her mother's cheek. "Yes, and thank you, Mama. I love you."

Then she did something Buddy Lee thought he'd never witness. She gave her daddy a bear hug the likes of which nearly knocked the man off his feet.

"With a little work, you just might make a passable granddaddy," Faith whispered, then kissed his wrinkled cheek.

"Hhmmmph," was the only reply Lionel made before his wife took his arm and marched him out the door.

His father-in-law sounded like he had something caught in his throat. Crow, maybe?

He wasn't quite sure what had just happened here, but when he also found himself the recipient of one of Faith's bear hugs, he figured the smartest thing was to go with the flow. He hugged her back, his heart just smiling all over the place.

Some days the alligators lost.

Buddy Lee viewed the meager excuse for dinner they'd managed to scrounge up and tried to quiet the grumbling in his stomach. There hadn't even been any TV dinners in the freezer. Grocery-shopping would definitely be a challenge for their little family, but that wasn't what was on his mind at the moment. Faith's earlier unexpected actions were.

They'd returned home from the courthouse, and after a quick inventory of their kitchen cupboards, had settled side by side on the lumpy, blue-plaid sofa, sharing a plate of chips and cheese. He'd found a root beer in the back of the fridge, and Faith drank a glass of milk.

"I can't believe you told your folks about the baby being Royce's."

There'd been a lot of things he hadn't believed about the events of the past few hours. Listening to Faith relate the humiliating details of her relationship with Royce to her folks and the deputy sheriff had been about as unbelievable as hearing Lionel Morgan admit to being wrong. He hadn't expected to live long enough to see either one happen.

Of course, for almost two weeks now, his life had been one unexpected hoo-ha after another. At least, thanks to Faith and her daddy, he wouldn't be spending the rest of it behind bars like his old man.

He took her hand, rubbed his thumb along the inside of her wrist. "Why did you do it, darlin'?"

Not sure what he hoped her answer would be, his breath lodged in his throat when her big, deep-as-the-sea green eyes roamed his face and settled on his mouth. He leaned forward, angled in for a kiss, and felt her fingers pluck at the corner of his lips. What the...?

She held up a thread of melted cheese and smiled a smile that buckled his knees. Good thing he was sitting down.

He swiped the back of his hand across his mouth. Jeez Looeeze! He felt like a toddler just learning to feed himself. It was damned hard to get serious with food hanging on his face.

Faith took a napkin and slowly rubbed it across his closed lips, following the seam into the corner of his mouth. The tip of her finger disappeared behind the napkin, stroking until he parted his lips to let her finger touch his tongue.

Her own tongue traced a wet circle around her mouth, just slowly enough to make him want to bash his head against the wall. Lightning rods of need drove into his groin. His hardness surged against the fly of his jeans again when Faith gave him the answer he'd been waiting for all his life.

"I did it because I love you, Buddy Lee. Don't you know that by now?"

Yeah, but why can't I believe her? He wanted to, more than anything in his messed up world. More than that, he wanted her to believe in him. Being grateful was fine, but it didn't go far in the way of loving.

He cupped her chin, tipped her face toward his and took the kiss he'd been after. Kissed her hard and shook clear to his shoes with the intensity of her response.

He forced himself to pull away from her exquisite mouth. "We have a lot of important stuff to talk about, Faith, but if we don't quit doin' this, we're never gonna get things settled between us."

"Are you saying this is wrong?"

Her puzzled look told him she didn't know what she did to him. Didn't have a clue. Or did she?

"No, not wrong. We're married. But it's wrong if you're only sleeping with me out of gratitude. What I said about not knowing how to love your baby...That's the truth. I don't. All I can promise is to try. If that's not enough and you want to leave after the baby's born, try to find a new life somewhere, I won't stop you."

He paused to grab a breath, then took both her hands and held them against his chest. "See how just being near you excites me, darlin'? I think you feel the same way, but there has to be more to our relationship than mind-boggling sex. I'm not complaining about that part, mind you, but we have to think about the future here."

"Sometimes, you're way too level-headed." Faith rubbed her palms over the soft chambray shirt covering his chest, slowly traced his taut abdomen, then tucked her fingertips inside the waistband of his jeans. "I'll admit I was grateful at first, and yes, I took your help for granted. But somewhere along the way, I realized my gratitude had changed to something deeper." She tugged him closer. "Something surprisingly wonderful."

"It did?" His heart leaped, did a crazy somersault, and landed back in his chest, amazingly intact. Did he dare to hope? His dreams had been shot down too many times not to be wary. When it came to fantasies of the heart, he'd learned to be pretty damn cautious.

Then she kissed him like there was no tomorrow, and Buddy Lee Walker threw caution to the wind.

Chapter Sixteen

On Friday, Scooter stopped by the shop to see if Buddy Lee wanted to go down to the courthouse with him. It seemed all of Liberty and half the county was turning out for the auction.

"No way," he answered emphatically. He had his own reasons for staying away, choosing instead to spend his Friday focusing on putting some cold cash in his bank account. The hardware store's beat-up van was waiting in the back bay for him to make it run another six months. Right. Everybody expected miracles.

But anything was better than watching while the Mustang he'd spent hundreds of hours restoring was driven away for a second and final time. That was *waaay* too much self-inflicted torture. He only hoped the new owner realized what that car was: a jewel of an automobile.

A feeling akin to deep grief settled in his gut, like he'd lost an old friend. . .And that was the dumbest thought he'd had in a long time. *It's just a damned car, Walker. Get over it!*

His life had changed so much in the past two weeks, he figured he ought to try selling it for a soap opera series. Maybe that'd put his finances back in the black. Or at least close enough to be gray.

He tossed a wrench on the workbench and dug for a bigger one in his tool box. Not finding one in the greasy pile of sockets, screwdrivers and drill bits, he heaved a sigh of resignation and treated himself to a cold root beer from the vending machine. Might's well accept the fact he'd never see that car again, unless someone from town bought it. Damn, he hoped that didn't happen, either. Seeing someone else behind the wheel would be torture.

Pulling the metal folding chair away from the wall, he spun it around and straddled it, arms crossed on the top. The can of root beer dangled from one hand. He glanced out the grimy front window just as a long, black Lincoln glided past. Lionel Morgan on his way to the auction to gloat, most likely.

He clenched his jaw and mentally ran through his entire collection of cuss words plus a few extra. Although they'd come to a sort of impasse over his marriage to Faith, his father-in-law still had an uncanny way of making him feel like a loser.

He stretched to turn on the small, dust-covered boom-box on the counter. While Vince Gill sang about having forever in mind, Buddy Lee chugged root beer and thought about his sweet wife. *Forever* was definitely in his mind just then. To say he was a lucky man was like saying rain was wet, no doubt. And who would've ever thought he'd be happily married to the woman of his dreams. Of course, the shadow darkening those dreams was the all-out fact that he was still a struggling mechanic with very few assets and a truck-load of debt. Boyd's boy wasn't quite a success yet and couldn't guarantee he ever would be. Was it fair to ask Faith to endure the only kind of life he had to offer?

He contemplated the alternatives and didn't like any of them. Life without Faith wasn't worth a plug nickel.

A commotion out front grabbed his attention as Scooter banged through the door, waving his arms like a windmill on fast-forward.

"B.L., you shoulda' been there. Sonuvagun, the bids went sky-high. Over the top, I tell you. That 'stang of yours was the star of the show. Y'oughta be right proud, all the work you done on her." He balled his fist and clobbered the pop machine a couple of times. "'Course, ol' Royce didn't have much in the way of assets. Some high-tech entertainment stuff. Not much else."

Buddy Lee tossed Scooter some change and nodded toward the battered dispenser. "Don't wreck the equipment," he mumbled, doing a piss-poor job of acting like he didn't care about the auction.

Scooter popped the top on his soda, launching into a detailed, bid-by-bid replay of the goings-on down at City Hall.

Buddy Lee thought he'd swallowed a crowbar, his chest ached so hard. "Who had the final bid?" The question slipped out before he caught it. *Gee, why not just ask to be crucified right here and now?* He tossed back more root beer to get rid of the crowbar. Didn't work.

"Not rightly for certain, but nobody from Liberty," Scooter assured him.

"How do you know that?" Maybe there was hope, after all. The car would have a new home far, far away.

"The bid was by phone. Can you beat that? The feller from the attorney's office was in touch with the bidder on his cell phone. Some people didn't think that was fair, but, shoot, if the guy wanted the car and had the money...." Scooter lifted his bony shoulders as if to say "Them that has, gets."

Buddy Lee's heart crawled back into place from somewhere down in his socks. Well, hell, that was that. He'd have to tell Faith now.

She'd stayed home, a wave of morning sickness laying her low for the day. Just as well. She didn't need the stress and disappointment of watching him lose the car to pay off Royce's debts. In fact, she'd almost insisted he stay at the shop until closing time. Said she needed absolute quiet to get over her wobbly feeling.

So, okay, but he still wanted to call and check on her. The phone wasn't in their bedroom, but she ought to be feeling better by now and, hopefully, would be up and about.

He dialed. Waited. Ten rings should have been enough to wake her if she was sleeping. He hung up and dialed again. *Must've dialed wrong the first time. Yeah, that's it.*

Ten more rings went unanswered and sweat popped out on Buddy Lee's forehead. Where was she? Had something happened and she couldn't get to the phone? A million scenarios shot across the video screen in his mind like the trailer for a suspense movie. He glanced at the wall clock. Nearly six. She should be home.

The phone bounced in its cradle when he dropped it. He slapped the light switches off, yanked the shop door shut, keyed the double-lock, and sprinted to his truck. In less time than it took to hiccup, he was squealing tires and burning rubber.

Scooter was left standing in front of the closed shop with a bewildered look and his mouth hanging open.

By the time Buddy Lee burst through the back door of his house, his heart was revved at maximum rpm's.

"Faith!" His shout echoed back at him from the walls, then died off in the empty room. Searching for evidence that she was still home, his glance landed on the kitchen counter. And another damned note.

With what breath he had left, he huffed out a shaky sigh of relief as he read the sketchy two-liner.

Buddy Lee, I felt better and went for a walk. I'm at Mama's. Please come and get me after you get cleaned up.

Faith.

Relief made his shoulders sag. She must be feeling better. And walking was good for her. Doc had told them that right from the beginning. He wished he'd had time to walk with her and promised himself he'd make time real soon.

Yanking his shirttail from his jeans, he headed for the shower. *Clean up.* Yeah, her hint was so obvious he almost chuckled. Mustn't go to the mansion in greasy duds. Wouldn't do.   He pulled his shoes off, shucked jeans, boxers and socks, and by the time he reached the bathroom was bare as the day he'd been introduced to the world.

That thought stopped him right in his tracks. Twenty-five years ago today, to be exact, but who besides himself knew that little bit of trivia? Not that it mattered.

He soaped up, scrubbed hard—even his greasy elbows— and dried off. Towel knotted at his waist, he shaved, after-shaved, deodorized, and tried to slick back his thick, wet hair. After brushing his teeth until they hurt, he donned clean jeans and a fresh sport shirt. Pondered the sinking feeling that had slammed into him when he entered his lonely house. Before he'd ever called out Faith's name, the hollowness in his gut told him she wasn't there.

He'd become attuned to her presence, her scent, and the playful way she pretended to be busy in the kitchen when he knew damn well she wasn't cooking anything. The way she laughed when he held up the take-out bag from the Pizza Palace or the Chinese restaurant just outside of town made his insides go all goofy. Sometimes, if he was lucky, she tempted him with a kiss hot enough to scorch the paint off the walls.

In his own unsophisticated way, he'd become accustomed to her in his life. When she wasn't by his side he missed her something fierce. Couldn't imagine how it would be without her. Sure as hell didn't want to find out.

He checked his image in the mirror over the dresser, finger-combed his damp hair and declared himself presentable, even for the Morgans. If he was lucky, they wouldn't be around, and he could hustle his wife back home. But when had *luck* ever been on his side?

Oh, stuff it, Walker. He shook his head to get rid of the self-pity keeping him company too much lately. He had Faith—the best thing that had ever happened to him—his loan had been extended to a doable deadline, his customers still straggled in to provide needed income. And he wasn't behind bars.

Luck had played a big role in his life lately, and he'd best remember that. Now if he could just get past the "baby" issue. But the knot in his gut still bunched into a fist when he thought about Royce...and Faith.

Pushing the whole complicated mess from his mind, he concentrated on the woman he loved. That was all that really mattered. Wasn't it?

When he pulled into the Morgans' drive, the unusual number of cars parked there caused a moment of panic but not surprise. Lionel and Beryl Morgan's social circle included county and state big shots, and the CEOs of corporations in Austin, San Antonio, Houston and Dallas. More than once, Faith had told him about all her parents' shindigs. Her stories made him glad he wasn't society material. Why the Morgans chose to remain in Liberty was something of a puzzle to him, but solving it was not on his list of things-to-do today. No sirree, he just wanted to collect his wife and go home.

The truck ticked the rear bumper of a green Taurus when he maneuvered into a tight parking spot, but thankfully, didn't leave any marks. He could almost swear the car belonged to Hap Donnelly, but that seemed highly unlikely. Taking a closer look at the array of parked cars, he thought it was damned strange that most of the vehicles were mid-size, family models. Not a stretch limo in sight. Hmmm.

He left his truck parked next to the green Taurus and made his way across the drive. Faith must not have known her folks were entertaining, or she'd never have walked over there. That's why she wanted him to come after her, he guessed.

He rang the doorbell and waited.

Watching guests mill about with drinks in their hands and awed looks on their faces, Faith paced near the mammoth stone fireplace gracing an entire wall of the sunken entertainment area of her parents' home.

For most of them, this was their first visit to the Morgan residence, and their heads swiveled like owls, trying to take in their surroundings in one glance.

Everyone who knew Buddy Lee had been invited, and Faith had made certain her daddy spoke to each and every person as they came through the front door. He'd grumbled something about being ordered around in his own house, but had finally given in.

Faith knew he was having a difficult time climbing off his high horse. He'd been up there too long to make the change overnight. But this party was the first step in his descent into the arena of common folks, and she was determined to see that he didn't falter.

"If you can't act like the gentleman I know you can be, you can't stay," she'd admonished him upon arriving earlier that day to make certain her directions for the party were carried out.

She knew him well enough to know he wasn't about to leave as long as he was footing the bill for the event. Remembering the sly way she and Mama had coaxed him into agreeing to pay for Buddy Lee's surprise birthday party, Faith smiled and hugged the memory to her heart. Daddy was coming around. Slowly, to be sure, but oh, how sweet it was to see him occasionally take a back seat to his wife's wishes when Beryl made them known. And her mama blossomed under his tender attention. How sad they'd wasted so many years, when they could've been bringing joy to each other. Faith didn't intend to make the same mistake.

As Buddy Lee's arrival drew closer, excitement bubbled inside her. She'd hoped he'd come earlier, but the guests didn't seem to mind waiting since food and good music were plentiful.

She'd given strict instructions to the hired D.J. to play nothing but country music, especially ballads. Her favorites—George Strait, Clint Black, Vince Gill and Mickey Gilley, to name a few. She could hardly wait to dance with her husband again.

The crowd spilled out into the evening, strolling around the swimming pool and gardens. A nearly full moon was guaranteed to appear later. She'd checked the calendar to make sure.

Lost in thought, she didn't notice Scooter's approach until his gravelly voice jarred her back into the moment.

"This beats all, Faith. You sure know how to throw a hum-dinger of a party." He carried a plate full of appetizers in one hand and a glass of sweet tea in the other. A wide grin split his face in two. "B.L. will sure be surprised when he gets a look-see at this." He waved the hand holding his glass in a sweeping arc to indicate the celebration. "I ain't never seen such fancy doin's. Nope, never."

"I'm glad you came, Scooter. I just hope Buddy Lee isn't too shocked. Do you think he'll like the idea?"

"Shoot, Faith, he'll be knocked cross-eyed. I know for a fact he's never had no kind of party, even as a kid." Grinning, he excused himself and headed through the open French doors out to where tables covered in party-colored toppers graced the perimeter of the pool.

Bright-colored balloons bobbed from lamp posts, and streamers in rainbow hues rippled in the gentle evening breeze. Tiny white party lights winked like fireflies from myriad strings draped over every archway and entwined through every tree close enough to cast shadows over the entire gala.

Faith watched Scooter take a seat beside one of his cronies from the GAS 'N GO and dive into his heaped-up plate. He'd never really said Buddy Lee would be happy about the party, just that he'd be knocked cross-eyed. That could mean most anything.

A tiny seed of doubt had popped up when the idea of giving him a birthday party first came to her, growing to bigger proportions these last few days as she finalized her plans. What if he didn't like what she'd done? Would he be angry? Embarrassed? Both?

They'd never talked about what really mattered in their new marriage. Never had the opportunity in the short two weeks since they'd said "I do." Suddenly, a wild possibility made her heart skip. What if he turned and walked out when he saw the crowd? Why hadn't she been more sensitive to his feelings? He'd been through so much lately. Given up more than he should have for her and the baby's welfare. Would her impulsiveness result in another bad decision? She only wanted to make everything right again. Why was that such a difficult thing to do?

Buddy Lee loved her, but would he regret marrying her after the baby arrived? He'd been honest about his feelings. She only hoped he could somehow put aside the ugly fact of the child's paternity. A lot to ask of any man. Too much to ask of the man who loved her and always had.

She remembered her shock when he'd revealed his feelings, but thinking back to all the times she'd selfishly turned to him for help, she realized it had been apparent to everyone but her. No wonder Daddy had forbidden her to have anything to do with *Boyd's boy.* Even he'd recognized what she'd failed to see.

A guest strolled by, spoke to her. Nerves a bundle of high-charged electrical wires, she answered absently. Paced some more. Checked her watch. Where was he?

She moved from the fireplace to a corner with a better view the front entryway. Another guest marveled at the beauty of the house, thanked her for the invitation and moved on. Faith couldn't have identified the person if her life had depended on it. The room blurred, started to spin, and suddenly, she knew she needed to sit down.

Swallowing hard, she asked a passing black-coated waiter for a glass of water. *Oh, please, not now,* she begged silently. *I can't pass out before Buddy Lee gets here.*

"Are you all right, dear?" Her mother appeared at her side, took her hand and led her to a chair.

"I forgot to eat," Faith admitted, blinking her eyes to ward off the dizziness. "I was so excited about the party, I didn't take time to fix anything."

"Never mind." Beryl Morgan patted her daughter's hand. "I'll bring you something as soon as I catch your daddy's eye. He can stay with you until I get back."

Seemingly in no time, Beryl had Lionel by the sleeve and was giving him an earful of instructions.

He sat next to Faith, then reaching awkwardly for her hand, cleared his throat. "You look pale. Should I get Doc

Sutter? He's over talking to Joe Bob." Definitely uncomfortable playing the dutiful father, Lionel's concern touched her shaky heart.

She shook her head. "I'll be fine as soon as I eat something." She sipped the cool water the waiter had brought. "It'll pass."

"Too much excitement," her daddy harrumphed. "You ought to be in bed. Need to take care of that little Morgan there." He nodded toward her still flat tummy, a faint blush creeping up his neck.

Though she felt weak as a kitten, determination stiffened her spine. Why couldn't she make him understand? If she hadn't felt so queasy, she might've stood up and stomped her foot. Not going to happen, though, unless she wanted to topple over.

"The baby will be a Walker, Daddy. Is that so hard for you to accept? Buddy Lee's a fine man, worthy of this whole town's respect. He's worked hard to overcome his daddy's reputation. How many of your colleagues could meet that challenge?"

She glanced around the room. Where was Buddy Lee? So many people were here to celebrate with him. Apprehension tied her stomach in knots so that when Beryl returned with a healthy-sized sandwich and a glass of milk, Faith could barely swallow.

"You have to eat, dear, for the baby's sake."

Her mama and daddy kept her company, watching every bite she took until they were satisfied she'd had sufficient nourishment. They hadn't been this concerned about her when she'd had the mumps. Her heart softened a bit. It wouldn't hurt to try harder to forgive them. After all, she had lots to be forgiven for, too. From her parents as well as her husband.

The front doorbell chimed, and her heart went wild. Her mama quickly shooed everyone into one big crowd, then nodded to the maid to answer the door. Faith held her breath as her husband's figure filled the doorway.

The crowd yelled "Surprise!" but Buddy Lee wasn't smiling.

Chapter Seventeen

"**H**appy Birthday," Faith cried and rushed forward, all vestiges of queasiness disappearing at the sight of him. "Are you surprised?"

She took his hand and pulled him toward the grinning crowd, knowing the question was dumb, but unable to come up with an intelligent sentence right then.

He had the stunned look of a deer caught in the headlights. She tugged his hand, but he held back, clearly confused.

"What's going on?" he muttered for her ears only.

"A birthday party, silly. For you." She squeezed his hand, laced her fingers through his and hoped her smile conveyed her happiness at being with him. Prayed he liked the surprise enough to not bolt out the door.

Buddy Lee couldn't speak. The crowbar in his throat suddenly reappeared, jabbing his heart, making speech impossible. His eyes stung and blood rushed through his veins as if pumped by nuclear turbines. The moment's intensity threatened to bring him to his knees, and he knew he was about to make a fool of himself in front of more people than he cared to count.

Gulping air, he scanned the cheering group. A birthday party. For him. For cryin' out loud!

Swept away by emotion he couldn't begin to identify, all he could managed was a mumbled, "Well, hell." So much for brilliant conversation.

Faith led him into the room, and the sea of faces swallowed him like high tide on the Gulf. By the time he'd had his hand shaken numb and his back slapped until it stung, he calculated he'd spoken to most every person in Liberty. He blamed his damp, blurry eyes for that.

But he hadn't talked to his father-in-law.

Not surprisingly, Lionel Morgan was nowhere in sight. He'd gone beyond anything in Buddy Lee's wildest imagination by affirming his alibi for the night of Royce Webb's murder. Showing up at a birthday party for a son-in-law he could barely tolerate was probably more than the old boy could stomach.

Buddy Lee didn't care, though. Right now, with Faith holding his hand and beaming up at him with that heart-melting smile, he figured he couldn't ask for more.

The friendliness of the folks extending their good wishes, like he was part of the community and not just *Boyd's boy*, dissolved the crowbar in his chest and a totally new feeling of belonging took its place. He was sure glad Faith had a firm grip on his hand to keep him anchored because he was on the verge of floating up to the ceiling and shouting "Hallelujah!"

Later, after he and Faith had eaten from the Texas-sized buffet and shared thick, gooey frosted slices of birthday cake, he led her out to the garden where a makeshift dance floor had been erected. Party lights twinkled like fairy dust, and the moon made its promised appearance, bright enough to illuminate the garden and transform the night into a lovers' paradise.

Slipping his arm around her waist, he drew her up against him and placed his mouth next to her cheek. "Why?"

His whisper brushed her skin and shivered along her nerve endings with mega-watt jolts of excitement. They swayed to the sensual voice of Charly McClain coming from the DJ's sound equipment, and Faith hoped Buddy Lee could tell how much she wanted him to surround her with love, as the song suggested. Her heart was so full, she couldn't speak.

"Why, darlin'?" he asked a second time.

Why, indeed? She wished he didn't need to ask. "Because I wanted to give you something special, something you've never had. Because I..."

She would've said more, but when he gazed down at her with desire glittering in his coffee-dark eyes and his mouth claimed hers, all rational thought vanished in moonlight.

She leaned into the man and the kiss with total abandonment. Forgot that they were in the middle of the dance floor. Being in Buddy Lee's arms was all that mattered.

Scooter cleared his throat and stood patiently waiting until his friend came up for air. "If y'all could leave go of that lip-lock for a minute or two, there's some people wantin' to talk to you, B.L."

Buddy Lee scowled. "You know, Craddock, you're a good friend and all, but your timing could sure use some work."

That remark assured Faith that her husband did indeed understand what she was saying—what she was promising—when she squeezed his hand and mouthed *Later,* then turned her attention to a very embarrassed Scooter.

"What people?" Buddy Lee asked before she could say a word.

Scooter jerked his thumb toward a small knot of people standing beside the DJ.

Faith recognized them immediately, but could tell Buddy Lee was puzzled. Smiling, she led him across the dance floor and had him stand in front of the group while she took a microphone and introduced them as the Liberty Country Chorus.

The three women and two men broke into a country swing version of "Happy Birthday" that had everyone cheering and singing along.

Faith swore she'd never seen such happiness as burst through the wide smile on Buddy Lee's face. The sparkle in his eyes looked a whole lot like unshed tears.

When the song ended and the clapping and shouting died down, she nodded to the D.J. Then as the sweet strains of Vince Gill's ballad about having forever in mind filled the warm night, she looped her arms around Buddy Lee's neck.

"Do you ever think about forever?"

"Aw, Faith, you know I do." His voice cracked.

So did Faith's heart.

"What about after the baby comes?" The minute the question spilled from her lips, she knew her timing was as bad as Scooter's. Buddy Lee's mouth formed a tight line and his body grew taut.

She hurried to cover her words, but it was too late to take them back. "I'm sorry. I shouldn't have asked. Not when we're celebrating your birthday. Forget I said anything."

But he couldn't forget in a million years. Her words had gone right to the core of his fear, and until he settled the nagging question of his ability to be a proper daddy to the child she carried, he'd never have her complete, unconditional love.

"I won't lie, darlin'. I don't know what kind of daddy I'll turn out to be, but I'll do my damndest to be good to the two of you. If that's not enough, tell me right now and I'll go."

His foolish, aching heart told him to cherish that moment and let the future take care of itself. He was scared of what lay ahead, scared of making the same mistakes his daddy'd made, but standing here with Faith in his arms, he knew building a family with this lovin' woman was more important than his fears.

The music ended, but the two stayed on the dance floor, oblivious to the sly glances of other couples waiting for the next song to begin. Nothing short of a Texas tornado could've torn their attention away from each other.

Then, Mickey Gilley's slow, sensual voice flowed over the swaying crowd like hot fudge syrup on cold ice cream, reminding them of all the things that really mattered.

Faith had chosen this particular ballad for a reason. As she moved into his embrace, she whispered, "You're all that matters to me, Buddy Lee."

He moved into his glide and slide, holding her close, unable to find words to express the enormous surge of love engulfing him. Tears of gratitude and love dampened his cheeks and he wasn't even ashamed. He pressed a kiss on the top of her head, inhaled her summer fragrance and sent a silent prayer to the Powers That Be for giving him this precious moment. This gift of love from Faith was everything he'd ever wanted. All he'd ever need.

The crowd parted and left the dance floor to watch the couple move together as if they were one in body and soul. Eyes closed, they swayed, spun and slow-danced until the song ended and the crowd erupted in loud cheers, applause, and a few risqué suggestions.

Buddy Lee was afraid he was blushing more than Faith, and *her* face was rosy-red.

"I guess now it's no secret how I feel about you." Faith grinned impishly. "Shall we tell everyone the party's over, and go home?"

"That's the best idea I've heard tonight." Buddy Lee swept her off the dance floor before the crowd got too enthusiastic. In his heart, he tried to sweep away the doubts of their future together, too.

Beryl Morgan appeared from across the room, face flushed and eyes shining. Lionel held her arm protectively, a totally uncharacteristic grin on his face.

"You look happy, Mama," Faith observed, eyebrow raised in question.

"Thank you, dear," Beryl said. "By the way, your father and I have something to tell you." She smiled at Lionel, but didn't give him an opportunity to explain. "The investigation at the bank has already been concluded, so your father's able to take some time away. We're going on an extended vacation next month—a few weeks in Europe to see the places I've always dreamed of visiting. I've already spoken to the doctor, who says the trip will be good for me and assures me you'll be fine, too, with Buddy Lee looking after you. Isn't that right, Lionel?"

Lionel nodded. "Whatever makes you happy, Beryl."

Faith looked at her daddy's silly grin and wondered what miracle had taken place in such a short time. She wasn't about to upset their plans by objecting, but she sincerely hoped her parents knew what they were doing. After all these years, it was strange to see them acting like they actually cared for each other. That would take some getting used to.

Buddy Lee stepped forward. "Don't worry about Faith. I'll take good care of her." He cleared his throat nervously, looking everywhere but at the older couple. "And by the way, thank you both for the party. It was a real surprise." He didn't know what else to say, not being good at thank-you's and never having had a birthday party before.

Lionel extended his hand, and Buddy hesitated only a second before taking it.

Faith's eyes grew misty watching the two men in her life shake hands.

Beryl kissed her son-in-law's cheek. "You can call me Mama Morgan, if you like."

Lionel harrumphed, as usual. "Well, don't be calling me Daddy, you hear?"

"As long as you don't call me Boyd's boy...sir."

The night of his twenty-fifth birthday would always be a night to remember for Buddy Lee Walker. In more ways than one. His emotions ping-ponged from the lowest point in his life when, after examining every possible option for solving his financial dilemma, he realized he would never achieve his dreams, to the ultimate high of the surprise celebration in his honor.

The mind-boggling realization that Faith had actually gone to the trouble of planning such an event just for him almost brought him to his knees. It sure as hell made his eyes watery and his insides go haywire.

Knowing she did so simply because she wanted to filled him with a heavy sense of guilt. How could he accept her love when that old alligator called *Jealousy* still snapped at his heels? He loved her more than life itself, but what if he turned out to be the same kind of no-account parent as his old man? What if he could never forget that Royce Webb was the baby's real daddy? There were no guarantees.

"Buddy Lee, are you coming to bed?" Faith called, her soft invitation breaking into his deep concentration.

Aw, shoot. How was he supposed to answer *that*?

He'd been reluctant to go to bed after they returned home from the party, knowing his emotions were pretty well warming up to high heat, so he'd worked hard at keeping her involved in conversation. True, it had been trivial chit-chat about the party, the folks who'd come to say "Hey," and of course, the peculiar way her parents had acted, but he'd managed to buy a little more time in order to snag his wandering good sense back to where it belonged. Not an easy task when his traitorous body had serious ideas of its own.

Earlier that night, he'd made a secret vow to stay away from Faith until he could deal with the fears still haunting him. She deserved total commitment, and he wasn't sure he could stick around after the baby's arrival, although he loved her so much he ached with an intensity that scared the livin' daylights out of him.

"Buddy Lee?" She stood in the hallway, silhouette outlined by the faint glow of the street light. "Is something wrong?"

Damn straight, he wanted to shout. *I have these gut-deep, uncontrollable feelings for you, and I don't want to share them with your baby.*

That made him a first-class jerk, didn't it? He'd already sampled the sweet love she offered. And hadn't he promised to take care of her and her child? Add liar to his list of short-comings. He never should have agreed to this wild scheme. Was something wrong? You damn betcha. The alligators were all over the place and catching up to him fast.

"Listen, Faith, maybe we'd better get something straight between us."

"Just as soon as you come to bed." Her teasing smile and soft laugh made her interpretation of his words pretty obvious. She wore the same flimsy blue thing again, the one that had shot his blood pressure off the charts in Mexico. He'd seen ads in magazines of those fancy underwear models, but they didn't hold a candle to Faith. Not even a flicker.

"I'm serious, darlin'." He tried to keep a straight face, but Jeez Looeeze! he sure enough wanted to howl at the moon.

"So am I, and don't ever forget it." She came to him then, looped her arms around his neck and leaned in until every one of her soft curves melted into his angled, hard body.

God, how he wanted her. It'd be so easy just to carry her back to bed and love the night away. He remembered the other times they'd made love and the wonder of discovery, the sweetness of surrender. Just thinking about giving up those blissful times nearly yanked his heart right out of his chest.

He groaned as he reached up to tug her hands away. God forgive him, he couldn't keep on this way. "I'm sorry, darlin', but this is never gonna work." At her look of utter confusion, he hurried to add, "I can't let you think I'm something I'm not. I thought I could take your baby as mine, but I'm afraid of what'll happen if I can't. That kid deserves a daddy he can look up to. One who can teach him important stuff kids need to know." He still held her hands, but moved a step back to put space between his eager body and her inviting one. "What if I can't be that kind of daddy? What if he's called *Walker's boy* and grows up despising the name? I don't want that for your baby."

He was only human, and right now he was dying inside. Walking away from the love of his life was the hardest thing he'd ever done. Maybe in time, she'd forgive him. Even if she didn't, he wished her happiness with someone else. *Like hell.* He closed his eyes and cursed the burning behind his eyelids that threatened to expose him as a weepy-dipstick.

With every fiber of his being, he fought for strength to do the right thing. Leave Faith and her child. Give up the right to her love, to build a future with her and have an honest-to-God family. He'd leave her his name for the baby's sake and hope it wasn't a mistake. She already owned his heart.

"What are you saying? That you're breaking your promise?" Panic stressed her voice to a thinly-veiled sob. "You can't leave now. We have everything all worked out."

She looked so bewildered, so vulnerable, he almost changed his mind. He cradled her face between his hands, and the tears on her cheeks slid between his fingers like warm, wet silk.

"Aw, Faith." Something painful tugged at his heart so hard he could barely breathe.

She lifted her face and stretched up on her tiptoes. "I love you, Buddy Lee. Please, don't be afraid for the baby. If I believe you'll make the best daddy ever, won't you stay?"

The kiss was there for the taking, but somebody was ramming a stake through his heart. He couldn't—wouldn't—put a child in jeopardy. *Boyd's boy* still lurked somewhere deep inside him, and those memories just wouldn't go away.

"You don't understand, darlin'. I love you too much to make your life miserable."

"That's just not true and you know it, Buddy Lee Walker."

The tears glistening in her emerald eyes joined sparks of gold fire. Her fingers teased open the buttons on his shirt one by one. He watched her temperament slowly morph from sweet to sassy. From dejected to determined. She was one hell of a woman, but his mind was made up. If he kissed her now, he'd never leave.

"Believe me, this is better for you and your baby. You'll thank me some day. And people will still think the baby's mine. I'll never say different. But he'll grow up a Morgan, and better for it."

"You're so very wrong, Buddy Lee. You aren't even giving this child a chance. You've judged and condemned without a fair trial. What gives you the right to decide what's best for me?"

"I can think of a number of times in the past...." He moved to capture her hands but they were already sliding inside his shirt, sending a message he had no trouble understanding. *Ahhh, sweet girl.*

"That was then. This is now." The sparks in her eyes flashed a no-nonsense warning as she got right in his face, put her soft lips next to his, and dared him to kiss her.

"Dammit, Faith," he growled," you're not playing fair." Having always been a sucker for a dare, he took charge of her mouth, kissed her hot and deep. Thoroughly. Definitely soul-shaking. *Mmmm.* He just might keep his mouth right where it was, rolling over hers, until life as he knew it came to a screeching halt. He tasted and teased, sipped and nipped, his tongue mating frantically with hers until kissing wasn't enough anymore, and he hauled her tight against his undeniable need.

She threw herself into the kiss with so much enthusiasm he barely managed to stay balanced and keep them from landing on the floor. So much for good intentions. He wasn't going anywhere —not now, not ever.

Pulling away from the kiss with downright painful reluctance as he gulped air to steady his runaway pulse, he knew he'd just been stripped of every bit of reasoning he possessed. He wouldn't have been surprised to find his brain in a jar for scientific study.

"Whooeee, darlin', you've got a helluva convincing argument." He started reviewing his previous decision with the two pitifully inadequate cylinders left in his think tank.

Faith favored him with that sweet smile again. The one that messed with his mind and encouraged the goofy notions of *forever* running rampant through his over-heated nervous system.

"This argument needs to be settled," she declared, "and obviously, you don't know how stubborn I can be when I decide I want something, or in this case, someone."

Oh, he was mighty aware of how stubborn she could be. Had discovered that little secret several years ago. Also understood why she nurtured that stubbornness. Protection for her heart. A disguise to hide her need to be loved. A cry for attention from parents with a bunch of mixed-up priorities who'd turned a blind eye to their only child's emotional needs in favor of social *hoop-tee-do*.

If Lionel and Beryl Morgan had indeed changed their conception of parental duties, Buddy Lee hoped Faith could finally experience the family love she longed for and deserved.

His own craving for love had nothing to do with his sorry excuse for a parent and everything to do with this woman he'd married. He'd entered into the marriage with only a teaspoonful of forethought simply because he'd loved Faith for as long as he could remember. She'd needed him and offered a chance to make his fantasy come true. In his rush to come to her aid, to protect her and be a hero, he'd lost his good sense.

The same thing had happened every time he'd jumped into the wild fracas of her rebel years, ready to bail her out of her most recent scrape. This undreamed-of predicament, however, had slapped him upside the head with reality.

The loss of his financial security, Faith's ex-fiancé's sudden death and the revelation of the abuse she'd endured, his near-miss of becoming a new roomie in the county jail, all made him take hard second thoughts about the future. Not to mention that, after all this time, she'd fallen in love with him.

The internal battle of do's and don'ts raging inside him was beginning to get a little lopsided, with the do's out-scoring the don'ts by a wide margin.

What's a guy to do? He regarded Faith with a war-weary heart. "I know your stubbornness first-hand, darlin'. I also know you're inclined to act first and think later."

"I've changed, Buddy Lee. Honestly. And I've given our situation a lot of thought." She took his hand, placed it on her tummy. "I want a chance for us to become a family. This baby deserves a chance, and I think you want that, too. This whole fiasco started for all the wrong reasons, and I take full responsibility for that, but look what we discovered. We love each other, don't we?"

He nodded. How could he deny the obvious, especially when Faith was looking at him with undisguised desire in her eyes? The emotion squeezing his throat nearly cut off his air supply.

His hand burned where it touched the softness of her belly. An innocent child grew there, one who had no choice but to accept them as parents. Was the deception fair to that child? Would resentment replace love as the years went by?

"Your problem is that you don't believe in yourself or that you could make a difference in someone's life," she told him. "This baby needs a loving family. Needs *us*. We can do this, Buddy Lee. Together."

Her hand slid under his, small and warm, and when she threaded her fingers through his, quiet strength flowed into his heart and soul, nourishing his starved spirit.

Give it up, Walker. Let go of the bitterness and quit making excuses for being a coward. Here was a chance to make his life count for something. What was he waiting for?

He folded her in his arms, felt her heartbeat join with his, and went for the gold.

"I'll try, darlin'. That's all I can promise. I'll need some help with the 'daddy' thing. What you see is what you get, but, I'll do my best to take care of both of you."

He knuckled her chin, tipped up her face. Gazed deeply into emerald eyes that saw beyond his upbringing. With raw emotion vibrating through every word, his mouth hovered over hers. "I love you, darlin'. Now and always."

She flung her arms around his neck and kissed him like there was no tomorrow. Oh, how he hoped for a million more.

They came up for air wearing silly grins. In between the wildly passionate kisses that followed, she managed to whisper, "And I love you back. That's all that really matters."

Damn straight.

He'd finally conquered the alligators.

Chapter Eighteen

When Buddy Lee opened the door the next evening and invited his in-laws inside, they'd been unusually good-natured, insisting they could only stay a few minutes because they were on the way to the airport. They'd decided not to wait to begin their vacation, and neither their daughter nor her husband wanted to discourage them.

Faith had offered her folks coffee, but they'd refused.

Now, the four of them stood at the back entry staring at the driveway. Three of them looked way too innocent when Buddy Lee pointed to the car and asked, "How the hell did that get here?"

They'd only been in the house fifteen minutes and he swore he hadn't heard any car come up the drive during that time. But, there it was. How? The car hadn't been anywhere in sight when the Morgans arrived. He'd have noticed his bright red Mustang, for cryin' out loud. He knew every inch of that car like he knew his own body.

"Well, now, maybe a genie in a bottle left it there for you," Faith's daddy said, avoiding his son-in-law's narrowed gaze.

"Yeah, right. Like I've got a magic lamp to rub." Buddy Lee raked his fingers through his hair. "I thought Scooter said somebody from out-of-town was the high bidder on it. And now it shows up here just as you're going on vacation? This isn't my first rodeo, folks. What's going on here?" He studied the exaggerated look of innocence on the three faces. Did he really look so gullible they thought he believed in miracles?

Beryl placed a soft hand on his arm. "Don't spend too much time trying to figure it all out, son. Sometimes, things have a way of working out that we aren't supposed to understand. That's what makes life interesting, don't you think?"

Faith gave her mama an exuberant hug. "Life certainly can't get much more interesting than ours. Guess what? A car collector in Houston called just this morning and asked Buddy Lee to restore a pair of antique cars for him. One will be delivered next week, so work can start work right away. The contract's very good, too. And the owner offered to carry the insurance. Isn't that great?"

Lionel cleared his throat. "Why, yes. Yes, it is. I wonder how he heard about your work?"

Buddy Lee felt three pairs of eyes staring at him, three faces looking suspiciously secretive. A trio of not-so-innocent partners in a devious plot to rescue his Mustang without his knowledge and find him more of the kind of work he loved. Lucrative work that would make it easier to take care of his new family. The damndest urge to hug all three of them suddenly threatened to make a fool of him. Wouldn't that shock the old man?

With a sly grin, he said, "I'm sure none of y'all have the slightest notion."

He should have been angry at being deceived, but somehow his new family's generosity kept him from wasting energy on resentment. Slowly, he was learning that he didn't have to conquer the world in order to rise above his past. Accepting his human failings and moving forward with life a little at a time had a helluva lot more possibilities for success. Maybe he'd make an okay daddy, after all. Boyd's boy was part of the past. He was his own man, now. No, he quickly corrected, he was Faith's man. Now and forever, Amen.

With Faith by his side, he would honor any debt his father-in-law might have incurred regarding the Mustang. Even if the old grouch did deny having a hand in its return.

Buddy Lee wrapped his arm around his wife's waist, fitted her close against his side. The sudden warmth sneaking in around the vicinity of his heart felt good, he admitted.

Faith laughed softly. "Anyone in town could've mentioned it, since everyone knows what talented hands you have." She slanted a heated look of longing at him. "With cars, I mean."

Suddenly, he couldn't get his in-laws out of the house fast enough. He thought about escorting them to the airport, but shook that idea out of his head fast. He didn't intend to waste a minute of his time with Faith after her parents took their leave. Which he wished they'd do pretty damn soon.

"'Bye," Faith called one last time as the black Lincoln pulled away from the drive. As soon as it disappeared down the street, she turned to slide her arms around him, her fingers tucked inside the waistband of his jeans. "I thought they'd never leave." She rested her head against his chest.

"Me, too." Cupping her face between his hands, he brought her mouth up and kissed her with every fiber of his being. He doubted he'd ever tire of kissing her. Of being with her. As his hands glided down to caress her curves, the two eagerly made their way into the house, anticipation hurrying them along.

Faith kept one hand anchored in the back of his jeans, her fingers stroking his bare skin and sending heated desire racing through his blood.

"Keep that up and we won't make it to the bedroom." The promise caught in his throat and came out on a raw whisper.

Faith smiled. "Oh, I'm counting on it." The tender love in her sparkling eyes went straight to his vulnerable heart.

As they passed through the tiny kitchen, he flicked on the well-used tape-player sitting next to the mismatched plastic glasses, empty TV dinner cartons and paper plates. Mickey Gilley sang to them about lonely nights, then softly crooned of love being all that mattered.

Buddy Lee understood clearly now. That's what love was all about. The total surrender of his heart with no holding back. The past, being *Boyd's boy*, Royce and Faith's relationship, none of that was important now. Loving Faith and the tiny baby who deserved a chance to have a real family—that was what truly mattered. This sweet woman, his wife, completed him in a way he could never have imagined if he lived to be a hundred and ten.

So, with sweet country love songs for inspiration, Buddy Lee Walker slow-danced with his beloved wife. Under the soft shadows of a big Texas moon, he loved her tenderly, and oh, so completely.

And when she loved him right back, he swore all the alligators grinned on their way back to the Louisiana swamps.

About the Author

Published romance author, Loralee Lillibridge, is a long-time fan of romance novels and a strong believer in the power of love.

Loralee grew up in Texas loving cowboys and rodeos, but relocated in Michigan after her marriage to a handsome Yankee who stole her heart.

She still favors country love songs, and seeing a field of Texas bluebonnets can make her cry, but she admits the West Michigan lakeshore has a beauty all its own.

Even as a child, Loralee's love of books, combined with a vivid imagination, fueled a desire to create her own stories with characters readers could care about. Her first attempt was a neighborhood play about a pirate who rescued a princess. (Original, yes?) Needless to say, the audience only consisted of her parents and the boy next door who reluctantly played the role of the pirate.

Now she enjoys writing emotionally fulfilling stories centered on the relationship of a man and a woman and their often rocky road to love. Heart-warming stories of ordinary people and extra-ordinary love.

She is also a founding member and past-president of the Mid-Michigan Chapter of RWA, a member of Published Authors Special Interest Chapter of RWA (PASIC) and Sisters in Crime. A native Texan, she and her husband make their home in West Michigan near their children and grandchildren.

This Texas flower credits her chapter and her wonderful critique partners for their unlimited support and encouragement on her roller-coaster ride to becoming a published romance author.

When not writing, Loralee enjoys reading, spending time with family and friends, and traveling. Visit Loralee at her Website or her Blog

Tell-Tale Publishing would like to thank you for your purchase. If you enjoyed this story by Loralee, visit our website to find more of her titles, or something from another of our wonderful authors. Remember to leave a review on Amazon and/or Goodreads. Loralee loves hearing from readers.